TRANSPORT

TRANSPORT

Peter Welmerink

Cover art: Jason C. Conley
Cover art in this book copyright © 2014 Jason C. Conley & Seventh Star
Press, LLC.

Interior Illustrations Tim Holtrop
Interior illustrations © 2014 Tim Holtrop
www.timholtrop.com

Editor: Rodney Carlstrom

Published by Seventh Star Press, LLC.

ISBN Number: 978-1-941706-03-9

Seventh Star Press
www.seventhstarpress.com
info@seventhstarpress.com

Publisher's Note:
Transport is a work of fiction. All names, characters, and places are the
product of the author's imagination, used in fictitious manner. Any
resemblances to actual persons, places, locales, events, etc. are purely
coincidental.

Printed in the United States of America

First Edition

Acknowledgements

Special thanks to Ken Campbell, Steven Shrewsbury, Tyson Mauermann, Tim Marquitz, Stephen Zimmer and Seventh Star Press, Julie Bonner-Williams, editor Rodney Carlstrom, cover artist Jason Conley and interior illo artist Tim Holtrop.

I would like to thank my family for being there, either in the background giving me time to tap at the keyboard, or listening to me try to explain what is this story I'm trying to tell.

Thank you all.

Dedication

This book is dedicated to my loving wife, Jenny, and my boys Christopher, Matthew and Aaron, for letting me feed the writing need in between all the bigger moments of this wonderful life with you.

This is also dedicated to my old hometown of Grand Rapids. You have filled me with a sense of happiness and adventure since Day One. May you continue to progress into an ever more vibrant place to work and live.

Weatherball blue, new strain of bird flu.
Weatherball green, more contagion foreseen.
Weatherball black, zombie attack.
Weatherball red, soon be part of the undead.

--Graffiti on the side of the Michigan National Bank Building, downtown Grand Rapids, posted in the Grand Rapids Herald, Sunday edition, September 2019

"*I will take the sun in my mouth and leap into the ripe air;*
Alive, with closed eyes, to dash against the darkness."
--E.E. Cummings

CHAPTER ONE
Gone Dead Train

The rail workers swung pick and sledgehammer, securing new spikes and tie plates as they worked new track sections into alignment. Echoing across the neighboring forest and field, upon every loud ping and clang of steel-striking-steel Captain Jake Billet winced. The activity didn't disturb him; the constant sound, the equivalent of a dinner bell being rung, distressed him.

He gripped his mounted Caliber-.50 machine gun, sure trouble was coming.

Swatting at a fly trying to land on his scar-striped face, Billet looked out around the flat countryside. West stood a sallow corn field, acre upon acre, stretching into the distance, separated by hedgerows of ancient trees and stone piles; tall weeds and grasses more prevalent than the rotting corn stalks. Unseasonably warm air for September gently breathed from the south, rustling the fields, making the dead stalks sway and rattle like a wind chime of dry bones. To the east reared heavy woods, a congestion of maples, oaks and pines so deep the recesses below the trees appeared black as night.

Standing in the forward command cupola of the massive M213 Ridgerunner-class Huron, he looked north down the vacant rail line, which cut the wilderness in half like a rusty steel blade. Nearly the size of a locomotive, the Heavy Transport Vehicle, or HTV, sat parked driver's side along the center of the train tracks and its opposite side wheels and massive treads almost to the outer edge of the ballast-rimmed rail line. The city of Grand Rapids, Billet's home base, lay 16 miles north, not far, yet felt uncomfortably out of reach even at that distance, especially sitting within a 72 ton armored strong box.

Behind him and the transport, railroad men worked the line. Looking south down the rail line—the deep secretive forest on one side, the tall dead fields on the other—sat the abandoned town of Moline, some of its buildings visible, sagging, leaning like they watched from afar…

…It made Billet right uneasy.

At one of the two rear rooftop ports, Lance Corporal Eddie Mulholland, thin as a rail with boyhood freckles still prevalent on his 24-year-old face, clasped a blade of grass between his thumbs. Leaning against the hatch coaming, he whistled a tune Billet couldn't place though the shrill sound from the gunner's makeshift instrument became increasingly annoying.

"Eddie, do you mind?" Jake said, reaching across and pounding his fist on the rooftop cargo doors to grab the young man's attention.

"Sorry, sir. Yes, sir." Mulholland snapped to, nearly bending himself straight over as he stood upright in his cupola. The blade of grass tumbled away with the light breeze as the soldier grabbed the grips of the Caliber-.30 mounted machine gun at his station.

Billet turned to the squat, hairy gunner directly across from his forward command post. Manning a quad Caliber-.30 machine gun with a 40mm belt-fed auto grenade launcher within its cluster, Sergeant James Stokes brought his full attention to what he was *supposed to be doing*. Almost losing his helmet in the transaction, he let a similar blade of grass drop from a failed attempt at whistling through it like his companion at the other end of the transport.

"Really?" Jake said, lifting a hand to bump his black beret a smidge from his forehead. He dabbed a dribble of sweat from his scar-laced skin. His crew had been extremely patient performing Overwatch in the heat of the humid overcast day as they waited for the rail men to complete the repair of several track and tie sections along the old Grand Rapids & Indiana Railroad line.

Activities were slowly taking place along several other rail lines running from Chicago to New Holland, and the Musketawa line from Muskegon to Walker. Once the main lines were again operational, opportunities for more goods in and out of Grand Rapids and West Michigan—including potential troop reinforcements and weaponry—could be possible. The G.R. & I. line, when deemed passable, would run again from Grand Rapids to Camp Wayland, to Kalamazoo and Fort Custer, all the way to Fort Wayne, Indiana.

"Keep your eyes peeled. With Mighty Mike working the sledgehammer," Billet said, nodding towards a behemoth rail worker who drove a spike into a tie plate. With one solid hit, it popped in like a loud metal firecracker, "any undesirables this far out will tune right in to us."

Mike Ferguson was the foreman running the rail crew. Solid as the sledge he carried, he towered over the line workers and kept at it as his five men hauled ties and steel plates, and muscled a length of rail when required. He knew the importance of getting the job done before sun down, and doing it right to avoid venturing out this way again. He also knew where he stood, keeping a .357 Colt Python at his hip and a M4 Carbine at his feet when swinging the hammer.

Out in the wilderness, beyond the shelter of large habitations like Grand Rapids, the undead populace roamed like wild dogs. Ferals, they were called. One, not a big deal: a pack of hungry, undead humanity, lots of trouble. The disregarded rural lands between G.R. and Fort Wayland held a surprising large amount of roving rotters.

"How's it going out there?" Billet radioed the rail foreman.

Jake watched the big man set the sledgehammer down on a newly placed rail, a few of his men checking the work along the tie plates and wood ties. "Alright here. That's about it for rail replacement. Got a few tie plates I noticed that need re-securing."

"You guys want to hump it a little faster. I want to get home before dark," Billet said, partially joking. If the rail crew was finished with the heavy stuff, and just needed to head back up the main line towards Grand Rapids, he had no doubt they'd be back within city limits before dusk.

"Roger that, sir-ah," Ferguson said with a mock-salute.

"Captain, you gotta listen to this," the Huron's driver, Lance Corporal Loutonia Phelps, said from below, calling up from the control cab. "They got Lettner ranting at city council."

Billet rolled his eyes. "Patch me in."

North Shore Coalition Muskegon Commissioner William Lettner, a mouthful of a title and a mouthy power hungry bastard of a man, had come to the city to discuss trade between the big lake shore region of the NSC and Grand Rapids. A large majority of inland folk disliked him as he enjoyed wagging his authority in one's face and openly took responsibility for an event that still twisted Jake's mind and heart. On this venture into the big city, his helicopter was crippled by ground gun fire and had to make an emergency landing. It crashed with no casualties except the machine, and, as the radio broadcast filled everyone's headsets, Lettner remained obviously none too happy about it.

"..personally hold Grand Rapids and its affiliates responsible for this atrocity until the guilty party or parties are brought to justice," Lettner's angry voice crackled in Jake's earbud.

"Atrocity?" Billet snarled. "You're one to cast stones, ya sonofabitch."

"...will continue to stalwartly pursue the elimination and cleansing of West Michigan even if I have to go beyond the governor, and straight to the East Coast Conglomerate."

Cleansing reverberated in Jake's head. His gaze dropped to the dog-eared picture of his wife and son taped to the under ring of his hatch coaming.

"Turn it off," Jake said, gnashing his teeth. "Whatever amateur shot his chopper down didn't use a big enough gun. Mother fucker, if he ever gets in my sights..."

The wind shifted. Billet crinkled his nose at the same time his gunners both caught the same rotten egg scent, scrunching their noses in disgust.

"Shit," Billet said grabbing his .50 Cal, swinging it around.

Mighty Mike sat in a half squat, one hand on his rifle, pistol already drawn; his men, and Billet and his gunners stood stock still.

Along the track line, a few yards from the rail men, the corn stalks waved and crackled at field's edge. A head emerged; flesh curled and gray, peeling like old dry paint. Where thinning scalp and sparse strands of greasy hair didn't cover, bare skull bone revealed itself. A rotting human thing drew out into the clearing, slowly, looking left, right, ahead. Nose just a shred of flesh, its black slits for nostrils sniffed at the air.

"Don't move," Billet said, mouthing the words without vocalizing them so as to not draw attention to him or the others. The rail men stood like statues.

The walking carcass, a Feral zombie, so decomposed it was sexless, pushed its way out of the field and started up the low embankment towards the tracks and the line workers. Another followed it from the field, and then another, putrid head rising, all sniffing the air like dogs. Those that had eyes were still sightless, the living orbs that had seen the world at one time were now glazed, milky.

The lead Feral zomb moved towards the rail foreman.

"Have 'em in the woods," Stokes whispered across from Billet, pivoting his quad guns towards the tree line opposite the fields.

Billet shifted his focus to the other side of the tracks where the tree line and underbrush nestled close to the ballast-heaped embankment.

A dozen Ferals teetered and shambled, all sniffing, snorting, as they emerged into the open. Seven came from the fields, and five from the woods. The corn stalks further behind the field group swayed and bent in different areas. And not from the stagnant breeze.

Billet squint into the dark depths of the forest, silhouettes of other flesh-chewers moved through the trees and brush in their direction. *Must have rang in every shambler in Allegan County*, Jake thought.

"Ain't no way they're all gonna hump it back here," Stokes whispered.

"Everyone's going home tonight," Jake replied without looking at the hairy gunner.

The lead Feral from the field drew up within a hands width from the rail foreman's chest. Mike Ferguson slowly lifted his .357. The creature sniffed the air, determining whether the thing in front of it was an easy meal.

Then Ferguson, in a half prone position, lost his balance and put his boot heel down. It crunched on the stones that made up the rail ballast. The Feral snapped its head, focused straight on the man. Its dry, cracked lips curled back, revealing broken, blackened teeth. Its skeletal fingers wiggled in excitement.

It found its prey.

Its head erupted in a red chunky mist behind the report of Eddie Mulholland's .30-Cal.

"Fire! Fire!" Billet raged as Stokes' quad barrels blazed, haphazardly spraying hot lead into the tree-clogged side of the tracks. Mulholland opened fire on the four remaining FZ's on the field side; one precision shot for each leaving a gristled stump for a neck. Like spooked deer, five more FZ's broke from the field's edge, though unlike the skiddish animals, the zombs came towards the noise, not away.

"Put a few grenade rounds into them?" Stokes yelled at Billet.

"Negative," he replied. "Use only in emergency. No slagging the rail crew."

Dropping into the Huron's insides, Jake found LCpl. Phelps leaning out of her cab seat.

"Orders?"

"Start creeping forward," he said to the woman. "Once we've got all the guys in, get us out of here."

Grabbing a machine gun from the onboard weapons stanchion, Billet ran to the rear of the transport, trying not to trip over the steel rails and other components the rail crew had stowed for the mission. The rear ramp had been opened for the rail crew to come and go as needed. Jake rushed to the open portal, readying to yell and flag the men back into the protective embrace of the Huron. The action died as the foreman and four others were swarmed.

Ferguson valiantly fought, firing the Magnum until it was spent, then using the M4 to club his attackers. He looked towards the transport, meeting Billet's horrified gaze before falling under a pile of clawing, biting Ferals.

Billet slapped the palm button to the left of the ramp. The big steel ramp groaned as the lip started to rise.

"Come on!" he yelled to the last man who stumbled, picked himself up, and ran for the back end of Huron. Jake fired at two zombs coming up the side of the embankment to flank the frantic, wild-eyed rail man.

A Feral suddenly appeared from the other side and before Jake could cut it down, it leapt onto the surprised man, clamping down on his neck. The weight and impact toppled the rail worker to the ground, his head bouncing off one side of the track. The FZ stilled the man's flailing with another deep bite to the throat.

"Damn it! Go, go, go!" Jake roared over the comm.

The Huron lurched forward, almost sending him careening into the slowly closing rear door. He found his balance and fired into the trailing zombs until the door ground shut before him.

"Jesus, man. They're coming out of the wood work," Stokes said, as Billet climbed back to his command cupola.

Billet kept his lower jaw from dropping. Breaking from field and woods spewed Ferals like angry bees from a hive.

"Mow 'em down," Jake said grabbing his .50.

All roof-mounted guns thundered as the Huron picked up speed. Phelps kept the rig at a steady 15 mph as beyond that the rattle and rumbling along the ties threatened to loosen bone from flesh.

"Can you smooth it out a bit?" Billet asked.

With a bit of explosive charge in her voice, Phelps replied, "I either put us in the ditch or put us in the woods. Your choice, sir."

A drainage gully furrowed the ground on the field side as they moved north; turning into it would spear the front end of the transport into the ground. The Huron could punch a path through the dense woodland but butting heads with a stubborn oak or maple could end that escape route.

"Hang on," she said over the comm.

The transport abruptly rose and fell several times. Billet peered over the Huron's side seeing track and wheels splattered with gore. He glanced forward. A tide of the gangly creatures flowed up from field and woods, spilling over the train tracks and into their path.

"This must be vacation land for every Zee in the state," Stokes shouted as he turned the quad's on the Ferals in front of them. He fired without aiming. The green-leafed trees not showing their autumnal colors yet suddenly sported deep crimson.

"I can turn off onto the road ahead," Phelps said through the comm. Looking at the GPS readout of her helmet's HUD, a paved county road was coming up within the next 1500 feet. "We have four miles until the 84th Street Outpost and the village of Byron Center."

Billet looked at the parade of Ferals following them. His .50 Cal was smoking hot, and Mulholland now took measured shots versus spewing a continuous onslaught of lead. He yelled at Stokes to pace himself, as the man would fire until his gun barrels turned molten.

Jake looked ahead as they rattled on. "We're not going to lead them to the outpost *or* the village," he said referring to the zombs who were still adding to their ranks as several others came from the forest line.

On their way out to Moline, along the rail line, they had passed an abandoned propone depot. Rows of rusting 475-gallon and 1000-gallon propane tanks lined a fenced in yard, including a huge main storage tank sitting close to the railroad tracks.

"Stokes. Eddie. Button things up," Jake ordered.

A good soldier, Mulholland heeded and dropped below, closing the hatch behind him.

Stokes noticed what Jake was looking at as they drew nearer to the tank yard. "Sir, is this a good idea?"

Billet glared at the sergeant. "Get below and get the burn salve ready."

"Jake, I can get us out of this," Phelps said in his ear bud. He could hear the worry in her voice.

The main storage tank is probably half empty or drained anyway. *This may be a worthless attempt,* he thought.

They rumbled by the yard.

A rusted sign hanging at an angle on the fence: *A-1 Propane. We have gas.*

Billet's Caliber .50 spit three hot rounds into the main storage tank as they cleared the yard. In answer to his shots, a massive explosion snapped him against his hatch ring, blasting the breath from his lungs as the tank blew. A second and third bright blast from some of the 1000-gallon tanks, obviously full, blew smaller tanks, fencing and large clumps of earth in all directions. The red-orange fireballs consumed the rail line, the field, the woods, and the Ferals behind them.

Making sure his spine was in one piece, Jake looked back as black smoke rose to the gray sky and flames crackled and popped all about the area. Caught in the direct blast, wood ties lay like discarded kindling, with rails twisted in and around them in haphazard steel braids.

"Shit," Jake said under his heaving breath.

Stokes and Mulholland opened their hatch and popped up like gophers.

"You okay, Cap?" Mulholland asked.

"I'm fine," Jake said. His forehead and cheeks burned as if he had pressed his face to a hot skillet and the hair of his scar-laced forearms lay in withered, burnt wisps.

Stokes saw the destroyed rail line, looked at Billet who gave him a fresh warning glare, and decided to keep further comments to himself.

The FZ line was dispersed. Mulholland sent a few rounds into some dazed stragglers.

The Huron hit the intersection where the rail line met the county road, and the HTV's front wheels squealed for a heartbeat as Phelps gunned it.

"Not to add insult to injury," Phelps said through the comm, "Got a message from HQ just now."

Billet lowered himself down into the bowels of the transport again, groaning as he felt the tenderness of bruised ribs after hitting the hatch coaming. He reached over to where the Lance Corporal waved a small wireless monitor towards him.

"Shit," he said again as he read the white font on the black screen. "Take us straight to the city, Lou. No stops."

Transport

Tomorrow was going to be a real bitch and, still watching the black smoke rolling towards the heavens from the detonated depot and railway, he hadn't felt the ass-chewing of today yet.

CHAPTER TWO
Road De-construction Ahead

"This is the Huron requesting update on Bridge Street OP status. We're right around the corner. Over," Jake said as he pressed the earbud in his right ear, making sure it was firmly in place. He stood in his commander's cupola, peering along the city street and down at the milling people. On this side of the dirt with beating heart and breathing lungs, they returned the look; some nodding friendly salutations, some turning away before eyes met, and others frowned and spoke in whispered tones to their neighbor.

"You think they know what we're hauling?" Stokes said resting a thick, hairy arm on the handle grip of his dual Caliber .30 machine guns. A ten foot span separated the two men with another two feet on the outside of their rooftop ports.

Adjusting his black beret—still smoke-crisp from yesterday's event—Billet winced at the gunner's question, not because of the question itself so much as the sergeant said it out loud *and* through his helmet mic.

He scowled at the sergeant, which crinkled the crisscross patchwork of scars adorning his face. The scar tissue lay the color of slender, light brown worms about his otherwise wind-chafed cheek, chin and neck. A series of scratch marks just under his left eye looked like a rough drawn three-pronged spear, the jagged points toward his hazel eyes. Two fresh red lines ran across the bridge of his nose, standing out slightly canted in center and to the right from an old break.

Noticing his captain's frown, Stokes realized his error and quickly tapped the receiver piece away from his mouth effectively deactivating it.

"Huron, this is Bridge Street Outpost. Lt. Danvers here. We're clear to the west, Captain. Just a few civilians waiting for lunch over there."

"Roger that, Lieutenant. We'll be at the gate shortly," Jake responded.

Taking up a lane and a half of northbound Monroe Avenue, the M213 HTV Ridgerunner-class Huron shook both street and building alike, as it moved towards the Michigan Street intersection and the Bridge Street Outpost. The twin Cummins V10 turbo diesels revved, belching thick plumes of black exhaust into the dirty gray September sky. The abused asphalt crackled and crunched under the crushing 72 tons of vehicle.

"We got some uglies following us," Lance Corporal Edddie Mulholland said over the comm in his thick Alabama drawl. He stood at his rear gunners post on the left side of the 32-foot long heavy transport vehicle. He manned a single tarp-wrapped .30-Cal. Unlike his squat gorilla-of-a-partner up in the forward gunners post, the young, lanky Southerner liked to keep his gear out of the elements until needed.

Billet glanced back over his shoulder. Though the streets were usually busy with the comings and goings of people doing their business within the walls of Grand Rapids Proper, he noticed a discernible pack of people wedging their way through the crowd of onlookers on the west side of the throughway.

"Trouble, Captain?" the voice of the Huron's driver, Lance

Corporal Loutonia Phelps, said from within the controls cab of the M213. "You want me to stop and see what they want?"

Jake could see the people, mostly men, carried thin wood posts with square sheets of poster board nailed to them. "Negative," he replied to Phelps. "Damn radicals," he said under his breath.

"Sure someone hasn't leaked the Intel?" Stokes said. Broadcast frequency channeled only to the vehicle occupants, the gunner still spoke too loudly, eliciting looks from people on the street.

"Sergeant," Billet grumbled.

"I can shoot him, Captain," Mulholland responded with a nod towards his front gunner friend.

Stokes raised a hairy fist and started to extend an equally hairy-knuckled middle finger.

"Speaking of which," Billet said to the sergeant who quickly reined in his improper salute to the rear gunner, "what's your weapon status?" He nodded towards Stokes' bristling quad gun cluster and the attached ammo canister.

"Only orange-tipped non-lethals, sir," the gunner said.

Billet raised a suspicious brow.

Stokes slid back the feeder bolt, peeked inside, and then racked the bolt back into position. "Non-lethals," he said as if proud of his find.

"No tracer rounds?" Billet asked. He hated harping on the man, but there were laws and compensation-draining fines for putting live rounds into the undead civilians across the river, and much heavier tolls for the living.

Stokes looked over his ammo canister. He shook his head, making his helmet rattle. "Negative. I know, I know. I learned my lesson from last time."

"I'll believe it when I see it, soldier," Billet responded, turning away so his deflated gunner couldn't see his grin. He did see the first person of the small throng raise his protest sign. The guy wore a black t-shirt with a picture of a family of four on the front, the script across the picture: CLOSE TO EXTINCTION. The sign he hefted and pumped in the air read: CITY FUNDS WASTED. GRCC. UCRA.

Another fellow lifted his sign upon noticing Jake looking their way. The man's sign, written out in black paint that had dripped while drying, read: SUPPORT FOR THE LIVING. NO UCRA.

"Unappreciative asses," Billet growled under his breath.

The GRCC—Grand Rapids Central Command—was the outfit he and several hundred other service men and women worked for. Besides Lansing and Muskegon, it was the biggest military outfit—a conglomeration of National Guard units and out-of-state armed forces regiments—centered in West Michigan. While they assisted the local law enforcement, they also did broader activities in and outside the city confines. The "shit work," as one of their prior commanding officers had poetically put it, which no one wanted to do and which usually required a bit more firepower.

The Urban Civilian Retention Area, UCRA, stood across the Grand River on the west side of town. Surrounded by the I-196 freeway on its north and west perimeters, and the swift flowing Grand River on its south and east, the UCRA was roughly three square miles of older neighborhoods consisting of ramshackle family dwellings and businesses no longer in use but utilized to harbor the cities undead populace. The majority of persons living within the secure heart of the city, including the mayor and most of his constituents, stood a very solid ground on the care and protection of their west side unliving neighbors; the unfortunate family, friends and other relations affected by the virus plaguing the world for the last twelve years since the 2013 H7N9 pandemic.

Billet watched the group of anti-zomb, anti-military protestors raise and wave their signs, Mister Extinction leading the pack. *There always had to be rabble-rousers.*

The Huron growled along Monroe, passing between the Devro Place Meyer Market and Living Center on the left, and the Grand Rapids City Hall and the former County Clerk Admin building on the right. No one really drove the city streets besides the police, fire and military. An occasional emergency vehicle ran as summoned from the huge hospital complex at the top of Michigan Street called Spectrum Hill. People on foot and bicycle lined the sidewalks and streets, going about their daily routines: working at small industries within city central, maintaining the municipality, tending the various gardens and food pantries. They kept an arms length distance from the massive tires and crushing tracks of the Huron as it rolled by.

"We have some activity on the other side of the street," Mulholland said, turning Jake and Stokes' attention to the east side of the avenue.

Much larger than the sign-toting people on the other side, Billet eyed the new group who pointed at the protesters and started across the roadway. The Huron jerked to a stop as the new throng crossed the path of the vehicle, their faces filled with disregard towards the hulking piece of machinery.

"Someone's gonna get a beat down," Stokes said giddy in anticipation of the two groups assured confrontation.

"Keep moving," Billet called down to LCpl. Phelps. They were already behind schedule not only with the late morning UCRA feed and surveillance run, but on getting their "special cargo" quietly, covertly and without harassment, out of town.

Something *tunged* off Billet's side of the transport, followed by another and then another, with the two gangs of men shouting as they merged together.

"Our land for the living!" Mister Extinction yelled in the face of a man wearing a loud sleeveless Hawaiian shirt leading the other gang.

Showing off his muscular arms, Loud Shirt had been shouting at the anti-sentiment group to go home before going nose-to-nose with Mister Extinction. "Our sisters, mothers, fathers and brothers

are out there," he responded referring to the citizens across the river in the UCRA.

Mister Extinction lowered his sign. "Bury 'em and move on with life, idiot."

His teeth were suddenly introduced to Loud Shirt's fist, and then both sides came to blows.

Billet had half a mind to keep moving as a crowd of onlookers gathered. He caught one of the sign-toters with blood running down the side of his mouth, stagger out of the mix, heft a rock from the landscaped ledge around Devros Place and throw it at the Huron. The rock struck the skirting of the vehicle—*tung*—and bounced off, hitting a child within the crowd of onlookers. The boy's mother scooped him up, and carried him from further harm. A man in the crowd shouted at the fighters and picked up his own rock and winged it into the combatants. Billet watched as a full-on melee broke out among the differing factions.

"Full stop," he ordered. Billet ducked as a rock flew over his head, bounced off the roof of the transport, clearing Stokes by inches. The gunner's gaze narrowed as he white-knuckling his quad gun.

Billet dipped down through the hatchway, and looked across Huron's dark bowels. Mulholland had done the same. Between them, a dark form moved within the crate-filled cargo hold. "Sit down!" Billet commanded of the figure. He called across to Mulholland who was strapping his helmet on over his short, straight blond hair, "Shotguns?"

Mulholland nodded.

Both men rose topside armed with a 12-gauge shotgun; Billet's a sawed-off double barrel.

Police sirens could be heard in the distance.

"Sergeant, quick warning shot, please."

"Yessir!" Stokes replied, swinging the quad barrel around towards the brawling gang. He squeezed the trigger, sending a loud salvo of rubber bullets over the heads of the milling crowd. The rounds hit an area of the Devros Place landscaping where a row of young apple trees stood. An aluminum sign explaining the trees as a recent addition by "the hard work of Ionia Avenue Day Care and Morton Home Senior Center" twisted off its fragile post by the buffet of bullets, and two of the four trees were violently pruned.

"Cease fire!" Billet exclaimed. He'd get a tongue-lashing from someone in the city council for this one.

From the opposite side of the street where an below-street level parking ramp yawned with its shadowy maw, two male figures emerged. Each wore a black handkerchief with a white skull design over their nose and mouth. They pushed through the onlookers, both pulling a glass Faygo pop bottle from a small rucksack each carried over shoulder. A strip of tattered cloth hung half outside the bottles and half within; the cloth within soaking up the liquid contents of the bottle. One of the men pulled a Zippo from his pocket and lit both cloth wicks. As the two men stopped and cocked back their throwing arms, bystanders standing close by backed away.

"Jesus!" Billet gasped as the sound of breaking glass and the *whoosh* of flame licked up the right side of the Huron.

Spinning the quad guns back around, Stokes reacted to the attack, unleashing a torrent of rubber brutality into the crowd.

"Kneecaps, kneecaps," Jake roared at the front gunner as screams rose and mingled against the rapid bark of the machine guns.

The fire hissed and drooled harmlessly down the side of the transport.

Mulholland sprang from the rear hatch, long low strides taking him across the transport's rooftop. Dropping down on one knee, grimacing slightly on impact against the black and forest green-striped metal surface, the skinny gunner snapped the shotgun into firing position intent on downing the Molotov cocktail-throwing assailants.

"Attackers ran back into their rabbit hole," Mulholland reported.

"They better not have ruined my baby's paint job," Phelps added from the Huron's cab.

GRPD cruisers barreled around the corner of Lyon Street onto Monroe; lights flashing, sirens wailing.

"Cease fire," Billet said, racking white-cased shells into his shotgun.

The machine gun fire ceased. The screaming and angry shouting and tumult did not.

Mister Extinction and Loud Shirt continued to flail at each other, their face, shirt and fists torn and bloody.

"Hey," Jake yelled, leaning over the side of the transport, almost out of his hatch, boot heels hooked against one of the cupola struts. "I said," he swung the shotgun towards Mister Extinction, a distance of maybe ten feet, and pulled the trigger, "Cease fire."

The gun boomed.

Mister Extinction went down.

Loud Shirt turned to run; same distance from Billet's smoking barrel. Jake racked another round. The shotgun thundered again. Shot in the back, Loud Shirt went face first to the pavement.

The quarrelers stopped, and the crowd dispersed as the police cars rolled up behind the towering HTV. Officers from the lead car jumped out of their vehicle, hands on sidearms and batons. An officer donning an arm badge signifying a sergeants rank rushed up to the side of the Huron as Billet pulled the shotgun to his chest.

"What's this about?" the police sergeant asked, looking to Billet and then down at Mister Extinction and Loud Shirt who lay moaning on the ground.

A small, unfurled bean bag lay beside each man. The two men would be sore and have a nasty welt where they'd been hit, but they'd live.

Hearing the grumble of his additional cargo, Billet used the butt of the shotgun to push back his sleeve and peer at his watch. He grumbled, letting the sleeve drop. He dropped the shotgun. It landed in the police sergeant's outstretched arms.

"Talk to those two when they've come around. You can deal with them," Jake said, casting a final glance at his victims. "We've got a feeding run to keep our *other* civilians from biting each other's heads off," he hesitated. "Unless you'd like to switch places."

***

Starting at the Bridge Street OP, the series of heavy chain link gates rattled to closed and locked position. Four such gates crossed the concrete bridge and roadway at every quarter span. Strung in great wicked spirals along the bridges side rails, concertina wire hummed as the cool breath of the river teased at it.

"We're clear," Billet said as the Huron cleared the last gate on the west side of the bridge. His team checked all sides of the transport, making sure none of the shambling civilians had wandered out of the enclosure.

"Roger that, Huron. Safe travels and see you back soon," Lt. Danvers replied back.

Jake didn't respond with the lieutenant's final words bouncing around in his head. He wasn't worried much on the direct job ahead, excursions in the UCRA were like breathing at this point. What lay beyond, however, what the men at the gate weren't privy to on this particular jaunt—the real mission ahead—was what subdued his response.

The final heavy chain link fence rattled shut like a rickety prison door behind them. The Huron commenced its slow trek into Grand Rapid's west side, the UCRA, lovingly called by those less enthusiastic, the *Undead* Civilian Retention Area.

Transport

***

Like a heavy thunderstorm quaking the earth, the heavy transport rumbled down the cracked and weed-festooned boulevard. Buildings and other structures, long since void of upkeep, shuddered and creaked as the massive vehicle went by. Billet was surprised the rotting tenements hadn't fallen on their heads during the history of the GRCC's excursions into the place. Some of the buildings and neighborhood residences had collapsed, the casualties only the already dead dwelling within—though the sentiments of the living relations were anything but that simple.

"They look rather hungry," Phelps said from her cabin control cubbie, the driver's viewport open fully to garner a better view of the area.

"Because we're late for lunch," Stokes said. He chewed a gristled stump of cigar fished from his pocket, his teeth stained yellow-brown with bits of tobacco caught along his gum line. He watched the denizens of this stretch of town sense their arrival. As the big rig trod along, the tattered, black-rot fleshed, milky-eyed unliving community slowly shuffled out and walked after them as if wading through molasses.

He ducked to avoid a stout tree limb caught and dragged along the Huron's roofline, the near one-story vehicle destructive even at that level. The main limbs skeletal branches snapped and harmlessly bounced off the HTV's battle-scarred but lovingly repaired armor hide as it crept through the dilapidated west side business district.

"If they get too close or look like they want to get a little reckless, toss them a few cans until we get to the MDZ," Billet said.

Like pets, maintained and designated feeding spots, Meat Drop Zones, were used every time. It helped keep tabs on the locals: who showed up, who didn't. It kept them centralized for the duration so other surveillance activities could be performed without interruption by a curious shambler.

23

The doped meat the UCRA civilians were fed kept them "docile" but it still hurt like a bugger even if they sniffed and nibbled.

"I'll prep some crates, and see how our passenger is doing. Call if you need me," Jake said, dropping down into the bowels of the transport.

The Huron started past an old adult theater, which had offered quarter peep shows and "toys" back in the day. Located next to a street corner, the two-story building still attracted unsavory types.

"There're my sweeties," Stokes said, chewing on the stump of cigar fervently. With one hand resting on the main grip of his quad .30's, the other tipped his helmet in brief salutation.

A gaggle of scantily dressed women, flesh rotting off their diseased carcasses, sat on the second floor roof awning of the old storefront. With their legs spread, they gurgled indecipherable sexual come-ons from partially hinged rouge-painted jaws. Their gestures were the only clue to their obscene propositions. With the HTV's roof standing in line with the awning, if such a silly thing wanted to be done, a good leap could land oneself in the lap of a rotting siren.

The gunner waved at the women, showing his robust arm. The sleeves of his combat coveralls were rolled up to his elbows, revealing limbs like a gorilla: the bushy, dark-haired arms a crisscross patchwork of white, raised scar tissue.

"Hello, ladies," he called, blowing them a kiss and wagging his tongue.

A tall brunette sat in the middle of the rooftop bunch, a real looker if the other half of her face was present. She waved back at Stokes with a right arm flinging bits of bloody flesh. Leaning out as the front gunner came in line with her, the woman made a sound like a wet, gravel-choked cough and spit a roiling dollop of chunky red-black phlegm at him.

Stokes flinched back and felt something splatter on the side of his helmet. He pressed his hand to the spot and flung off a meaty bit of what appeared to be the woman's tongue.

"Nasty harpies," the sergeant snarled.

The rotting succubus's wetly giggled. One showing more skull than scalp lost her balance and went sidelong off the awning, landing headfirst with a meaty *th-whop* on the concrete below.

The right side of the transport bucked. Its 32-inch front dualies, followed by its thick, black rear tracks, rolled over, and then bit down, into a rusted Buick sitting curbside. The old vehicle flattened with a metallic squeal and crunch. From a tumbledown home with a dirt lawn and an old maple tree whose trunk looked gnawed, a man loped from the doorway,; his skin as tattered and torn as his dirty clothing. His arms were shattered stumps at the shoulder, yet his gesturing and loud growls made him appear he was yelling and shaking a fist at the Huron for running over his car.

"Aww, shaddup, or I'll stump your lower body to match your upper." Stokes shouted at the rotting man, swinging the big guns around. Taking aim, the gunner was surprised when the zomb appeared fearful, turned and hobbled back into the house. "Huh. Perhaps eatin' brains gives' em a bit of brains."

"Gawddamnit, Lou, watch the road!" Jake yelled from below as he pushed himself from one of the steel ribs framing the interior of the transport. He wasn't facing the driver's door when he bellowed, but his words filled the entire chamber.

With weather-cracked fingers, he rubbed a raised lump on the side of his scar-laced chin, gingerly touching the tender spot. He'd have a nice bruise where he'd hit the bulkhead.

"Parking meter expired," Loutonia called back. "Sorry, Captain, roads supposed to be clear." Her agitated tone didn't sound apologetic.

Billet turned to the two men seated in the large open cargo hold: Eddie Mulholland and their "special" cargo: NSC Grand Muskegon Commissioner William Lettner. The North Shore

Coalition official sat holding the back of his bald head with one hand. He looked rather pissed and waved Mulholland away as the lanky gunner clumsily tried to help him.

"Do you offer this to all your visiting dignitaries, Captain?" Lettner said, bringing his right hand round to peer at it. His fingers showed a smear of blood. He touched the torn lump where his head had cracked against the back of his seat pan.

"First you let my helicopter get shot down," the Commissioner said, sarcasm and venom in every word, "You take all morning getting this pile of junk running while I sit in some hot, dark office waiting. You let us get accosted by the heathens of your wonderful city, and then you try scrambling my brains within this iron coffin."

Billet agreed they had started a bit late in the day for an excursion out of town. The helicopter incident was still under investigation, but whoever had tried had miserably failed in his book. The little Exiting Town fiasco seemed more and more common place, and a sign of the times, much to his dismay. Other than that, Jake could care less for the man's bitching. Visions of unholstering his sidearm, caving the man's skull and dumping the carcass outside for the "locals" to dine upon entered his mind.

Thinking better of it, Billet let his hand move back to steady himself against the wall of the vehicle as Phelps brought the speed up from a tortoise pace to a horse trot. The heavy transport could top out at 52 mph on pavement, but Phelps kept the speed subdued on city streets. She knew better than to roll over anyone teetering into the boulevard. The City enjoyed taking money away from the GRCC as much as they liked giving it to them for services rendered. *You can guard the chicken coop but if you step on an egg, be prepared to pay,* Jake reflected.

"We still don't have the Intel back regarding who shot your bird down," Jake began.

The commissioner glared at him anew.

"If I had my way I would have stayed far away from Grand

Rapids and this inland cesspool. Retention center for your diseased. Please. I don't know how you people can breathe this wretchedness. If Mayor Honeywell had half a brain, he'd scour a wider patch of land like we did and get rid of some of these worthless graveyard escapees."

Billet's jaw clenched so tight it was a wonder his teeth didn't bust out of his scar-striped face. His hand dropped to hang beside his pistol.

"You can use the head in the back to clean up and get Eddie here to patch you up when you're through," he said, nodding his head toward the rear of the vehicle.

Lettner unbuckled, stood, looked at Mulholland warily, and used his hands to steady himself as the Huron lurched and shuddered. "I'll be adding this to my report, Commander."

"Yes, sir," Jake responded.

Lettner looked at him, inspecting him for the slightest insolence.

Billet wore a poker face.

***

The Commissioner started his walk rearward, teetering like a drunk with the movement of the vehicle beneath his feet. Jake and Mulholland watched the man make his way to the closet-sized restroom. Lettner slammed the door behind him upon entering.

"He's a nice fella, ain't he," the young soldier said. He absently scratched at a slender red scar on the right side of his face running from temple to jaw. "Gotta wonder how he can have captivated so many folk and they treat him like some world ruler."

Billet chewed his lip to avoid voicing what he really wanted to say.

"It's easy to be the man on top when your peers and opponents seem to vanish every time you do a 'cleansing' through your territory." Billet said watching the door to the privy.

The tall, lean gunner seemed stuck wondering on the mysteries of Jake's statement. Poor kid wasn't worldly wise yet but a hell of a sharpshooter. His gun skills put to shame seasoned vets. Phelps was teaching him some mechanical aptitude also as two heads were better than one when the big rig broke down.

Mulholland's far away gaze could have burned a hole through the thick bulkhead. "I miss going out to the beach."

"You go every time we make a haul out there," Jake reminded him.

The transport thumped over something else. Lettner's muffled cursing sounded from the rear of the vehicle.

"Ain't like it used to be. Other than the preserves in Greater Muskegon and Grand Haven, the flora and fauna is the same sickly color as the dead folk *they* are trying to scour the land of," Mulholland said.

Jake didn't respond. He knew the young soldier spoke true and held the same concerns of what the North Shore Coalition, governed by Lettner, was doing to the lake shore. The bio-chemical agent they'd used to decimate the zombie populace contaminated the land and even its living inhabitants. Overseeing a large quadrant of inland territories, it was a big reason the Mayor of Grand Rapids constantly petitioned (and won) against "cleansing" the areas around the big city and surrounding inland area. The man knew the results.

The mayor looked out for his citizens, both living and unliving. A majority of the zombie faction just outside downtown central used to be living, breathing citizens of Grand Rapids, or its neighboring towns and villages. Surviving friends and family members still concerned for their kin who had succumb didn't want to see these poor wretches abandoned or killed so mercilessly. The mayor held compassion for the blighted folk, while Lettner openly looked to put down the afflicted as if they were simply diseased animals.

Billet found his hand wrapped about the pistol grip of his Sig Sauer M11, thinking of his late wife and son. His eyes locked on the door to the head.

How easy it would be.

"Commander, we're coming up on the gas station," Loutonia called from the cab.

Lettner stepped out of the head, and stopped. "Gas station?" He responded perplexed. "You didn't fuel up before we left? And you're fueling up...out here? Jeezuz H! You clowns aren't lacking on surprises. Tack on another fine missive to your superiors."

Billet ignored him, his sneer turning into a smirk. He stepped closer to the cab, gripping the doorframe as he peered in.

"Is Bob out there?" Jake asked.

Loutonia kept the steering column steady in hand, taking her foot off the accelerator. The massive twin diesels seethed from a thundering growl to a gravelly purr. Face pressed to the goggle-shaped driver's port, Loutonia answered. "Ol' Bob's out. He sees us. He's waving. That's always damn creepy."

Jake inched his way into the cramped driver's compartment. He glanced through the port as his driver sat back and slowed the vehicle further.

"I think he's lost a few fingers since last visit," he said matter of fact. "Yeah. That arm. We better tape it up before he loses that too."

Dressed in tattered blue coveralls smeared with dried blood, dirt, oil, and small chunky bits of ...something, stood a bow-backed, undead man in front of a defunct Marathon gas station on the corner of Bridge and Indiana. A small, white brick building in its heyday, the service station behind the rotting man now a weathered husk of its former self. Its white paint peeling, exposing red brick, it looked as diseased as its teetering owner. A service bay with a shattered wood garage door stood with dirt-fogged windows. There were two aged gas pumps, in the same decrepit shape as the building, with rotting hoses.

"Make sure the area is secure and come to full stop," Jake said letting Loutonia resume the drivers view port. "Mulholland and Stokes on guns, on point."

"As usual, Cap'n," came Stokes muffled voice from above.

Lettner pulled away from a side viewport and looked at Billet. "Um, there's a rotter out there."

Jake stepped aside to let Mulholland climb up into the secondary roof-mounted gun port. The engines simmered as the vehicle gently lurched to a halt.

"Yup." Jake said with a smile. "We get Intel on the happenings outside town from him."

Lettner opened his mouth, but no words came out.

***

Billet stood by the rear ramp as it lowered, letting the gray light from outside filter into the black insides of the transport. His dull blue eyes scanned the interior of the carrier. Along the massive steel ribbed guts, an assortment of weapons, ammunition and supplies stood securely strapped. A dozen large wood crates just beyond the john and before the large rear hatch were held in place by thick tie-downs. Keeping his pistol under one arm, Jake undid the strap to a singular crate and lifted the lid.

"Really? You're going out there?" Lettner said, moving up cautiously beside Billet.

Removing two small, unlabeled aluminum canisters from the crate, Jake dropped the lid and re-secured it. As the rear ramp moaned under dusty gears and dropped with a heavy metal *tong* upon the weed-festooned pavement, he checked his sidearm with one hand and held the two canned goods in the other.

"Since no one has figured out how they communicate amongst each other—either by a form of group telepathy or something else—we've found the easiest way to talk to our domesticated shamblers is to simply communicate one on one with them." Billet spoke matter-of-factly as the commissioner surely knew all this.

Lettner's eyes dropped to the canned goods Billet held, realizing their contents.

"So you barter with them?" The commissioner said. His face pinched in disgust.

"I suppose you could call it that. Better than not knowing what is going on, shooting them in the head and walking into an ambush out in the wilds. An eye for an eye," Billet said, glancing round the corner of the open ramp, looking left, right and down the street. "Or in this case," he wagged the two cans, "Intel for a few cans of processed gray matter."

Lettner further sneered. "Spam. Bram. Whatever you call it. This entire process should be outlawed. You need a translator even to understand what the cursed things are grunting and groaning about."

Slender fingers clamped onto the commissioners shoulder, giving it a squeeze to an almost painful point. Lettner stepped aside as Lance Corporal Loutonia Phelps nearly shoved him aside.

"I am schooled in many dialects, including Zomb," the dark-skinned driver said.

Lettner hadn't been formerly introduced as the young woman had been in the transport's driver's seat since he boarded. His look of disgust changed to one of astonishment and some sordid attraction upon seeing the soldier full on. Her khaki coveralls hugged flaring hips and full round buttocks. Her camo uniform top pulled taut against her large breasts. She did not button her collar; underneath a grimy tshirt rode to her neckline.

He noticed the two .45's holstered at her hip and decided to keep his gaze eye level.

Phelps ignored the man as she grabbed one of the 70 pound crates *easily* with one solid arm. She dragged it down the ramp, stopping beside Billet when she stepped onto the pavement.

"Unless you're interested in talking to Bob, I suggest returning to your seat...sir." Jake said nodding to Lettner.

Eyes still on Phelps, the regent turned and disappeared into the shadows of the transport.

"He's married, right?" Loutonia asked warily, raising an eyebrow.

"Was, but last report is sketchy. Running joke is he dumped her in the last dusting run like he supposedly did with a few of his council opponents."

Phelps looked directly at Jake. They exchanged the same hard-eyed look as she nodded.

***

Billet and Phelps moved with deliberate steps around the big transport. The sound and scent of the vehicle always attracted folk of both living and undead nature: wasting time out in the open not a favorable activity. And Zombie Bob, the service station attendant, known for snail-paced recitals of his knowledge, especially when decayed synapses fired at the level of a dead battery.

The service station stood on the south side of the street. Phelps dragged the wood crate several yards from the transport and left it by its lonesome in the center of Indiana Avenue, the side street which the bulk of the Huron blocked. Glancing up at Mulholland at the left front gun, she exchanged thumbs up with the lanky soldier.

"Hello, Bob." Billet said, not shouting as he stood only two feet away from the other man. With his hand on his holstered sidearm, he looked at the old undead service station attendant who still continued to wave at the HTV and the street.

Jake didn't know how long "Bob" had been part of the neighborhood. He'd been at the service station location as long as they'd been making runs from Grand Rapids proper; roughly eight years. From the reports acquired on Bob's history, the old zomb appeared at the service station a few years after the initial virus and contagion. From the decayed look of the man, he must have been one of the Risen, crawled from his grave, and resumed his unlife where he once worked.

After all the years of interaction, Jake felt Bob as an old friend.

Bob was also found to be a "satellite zombie." For whatever reason, he and a score of other rotters shared the innate ability to communicate—no one was sure, telepathically?—and retain knowledge regarding activities of other groups of undead both in the city and in the wilds. Bob and his special brethren were held in high regard considering their non-living status, something that kept them from getting their heads blown off when things slipped into chaos.

Suddenly letting his arm drop, turning his death-clouded eyes towards Billet, Bob sniffed the air, sensing the living man standing beside him.

"Whoa there, friend, it's your Ol' buddy Captain Billet." Jake said, quickly popping the top of one of the cans he held. He put it out before Bob's exposed nasal cavities: his actual nose long since rotted off his face.

Smelling the can of "brains," Bob lifted his hands to take the container. The arm he'd used for waving folded backwards, ready to slip out of the shredded moth-eaten sleeve of his coveralls.

"Hold on, old man." Jake said, taking a strip of the hanging coverall and tearing off roughly one foot of material. Bob sniffed at him, not at the can of fake skull meat. Where one might've very quickly found him or herself a chew toy for performing such an act, Bob recognized who stood before him by an acute sense of smell, and a few synapses finally firing.

Jake wrapped the cloth around the loose elbow joint. When he removed his hands, Bob seemed to respond by lifting his bandaged limb. It no longer flopped, but stood rigid. His future waving endeavors would come off a bit stiff, though better than his arm coming off.

"Got some civilians way down the street, but not sure if they sense us or are just random walkers," Loutonia said as she approached Billet and Bob. "Hey, Bob."

Bob sniffed at her. She didn't move to stop him, knowing the ritual.

"We're going west, out along route M-45," Jake said to the man. The zomb service station attendant's head jerked upwards as if each word slapped him. "What do we have to look forward to? We heard there was some trouble out at the old university causing trouble for the homesteaders out beyond Allendale."

Bob's head dropped to his chest on Billet's last word. For a moment it looked as if someone flicked his switch off.

Phelps glanced over Bob's shoulder, warily eyeing the defunct service stations interior and the area beyond.

Billet looked in the other direction, down the way they'd come. He could see loping figures many blocks away, though they seemed to be staying put. He shot a glance to the Huron, Stokes and Mulholland dutifully watched them. They gave him a nod: nothing coming their way…. yet.

"Any time now, Bob." Billet growled lowly, anxious to be moving on.

It didn't matter how you were loaded out, or how good a rolling armored shelter you had. The undead far outnumbered the living. They could reduce your weapons to drained magazines and make your shelter a coffin: a reality *always* on Billet's mind and at the forefront of his command.

Bob's head jerked upward, startling Jake.

Mumbling unidentifiable words, Bob drooled a line of bloody spittle to punctuate his statement. He moved his hands and arms about as if mired in molasses, yet with gestures like a frustrated mute explaining something, trying to get his point across.

Phelps leaned in, listening to the gurgles and halting grunts and groans.

She interpreted: "Marauders detonated…section of Interstate 96…between Coopersville and Nunica…"

"Yes. Old news. Two year old news." Billet responded. He thought he saw a curtain move in a second floor window of the sagging house across the street.

"Current news. M-45. Between Grand Rapids and Grand Haven," Billet said at Bob who continued to grumble and gesture. He knew it took a while for those rotted cogs to turn in the undead man's head.

Jake looked up at that same window again. This time he watched as the tattered curtain fall back into place.

Bob coughed violently, and continued "talking."

Loutonia continued to listen with a grimace, wiping foul spittle from the front of her uniform.

"Lots of activity beyond Reganshire," she said. "Residents from…the Valley State University commune harassing…friends. They have a new…mascot."

Billet looked at his driver with a sideways tilt of his head. "I get the VSU communal and the feral zombies out there, fighting, but new mascot? What the hell does that mean?"

Valley State University Bulls was the old university's basketball team that'd gone down in local history books as undefeated back in the days before the world stuck its head in the toilet and vomited forth the diseased state of things. A costumed guy in a cartoon-looking bull's head with a goofy snarl upon its fake fur countenance came to mind, donned in a puffed out and padded red and yellow sports jersey. Billet couldn't figure what "new mascot" meant, though knowing the VSU communal dregs were led by several nut job geneticists, he didn't want to think about the implications at the moment.

Movement caught Jake's eye in the second floor window again. He glanced up, seeing faces peering at him. Blood-smeared faces.

Unhinged jaws with broken, sharp teeth. They pulled away when they noticed him noticing them, leaving their grotesque imprint on the dirty glass like a bloody hand on a fogged mirror.

"Time to go!" Jake said to Phelps, tugging her sleeve and pointing to the group of "civilians" coming out the side door of the house.

The local undead populace might be "domesticated," but they still were always hungry.

Bob grunted, growled, and made a sound as if he was clearing his throat. It came out as a wet, long gurgle, and yellow pus oozed out the corner of his lop-sided mouth.

"He says he has a special on a lube and oil change," Loutonia ended.

"See ya, Bob," Billet called out, as they double-timed it to the transport.

Stokes and Mulholland trained their guns on the advancing walkers.

Jake gave Bob one last look before he stepped around the rear of the vehicle.

The old zombie gas station attendant was waving again, as if they'd just arrived.

***

"Light it up!" Jake yelled to the men topside. He passed Lettner who looked rather harried. "Don't worry, boss, everything is under control."

Lettner stood and went to the left side portal. He sucked in his breath, and glanced back at the slowly rising steel ramp. It creaked and clanked in protest, not promising to fully close before the diseased rotters made the transport.

The twin diesels roared to life. As the HTV lurched forward, Lettner grabbed the bulkhead to avoid being thrown to the hard steel floor.

Machine gun fire erupted above him. He peered out the small oval port, expecting to see the dozen closing zombies cut in half by the hail of lead. Instead, he saw the fractured roadbed burp clouds of dust beside the crate Phelps had dragged outside. The zombies hesitated for a moment.

"More of the neighborhood heading this way," Billet shouted from the cab. "Stokes, keep eyes forward. Mulholland, serve 'em lunch."

The bark of a singular Caliber-.30 machine gun sounded and this time Lettner saw the crate take the hits. The box flew to pieces, throwing wood splinters and its contents into the path and faces of the walkers. The canned goods, similar to the few Billet had pulled, went everywhere, including their grayish mess of glop. Some of the zombies slipped and fell, while others stopped at the scent of the "fresh meat." They dropped and raked through the ruptured cans and slop as if animals who hadn't eaten in decades.

None pursued the exiting transport.

Jake stepped from the driver's compartment.

"You squander bullets on shooting cans, not on pulverizing those monsters." Lettner said, wagging a finger at him. "Waste of ammunition. And you got a gunner up there who couldn't hit the broad side of a—"

Stokes squatted down from his perch. "Hey, fuck y—"

Jake smacked his fist against the boot of the stumpy gunner, shutting him up.

"We fire rubber rounds while in here, and we don't shoot 'em if we don't have to. Some of us still have friends and family in these neighborhoods. Flesh-eating, brain-rotted *monsters* maybe, but the mayor and the other city folk aren't real friendly to us if we go punchin' holes through the UCRA civilians," Billet informed Lettner. "Buckle up, Commissioner. It's a bumpy ride to the outer gate."

Lettner huffed and sat down in the nearest seat. Clumsily he snapped himself into the five-point harness, still cursing under his breath.

It further stoked Billet's fiery ire for the man.

"And I'd be careful on cutting down my crew." Billet said leaning in close so only Lettner could hear his words. "We have a long way to go to get you home. The sergeant up there has plenty experience putting a bullet where the sun don't shine."

"Are you threatening me?" Lettner spat.

Jake straightened, turned and went back to the driver's compartment. He thought he'd find mirth in imagining Lettner crated up and Stokes taking potshots at him, but the irritation with the man—and the item the NSC commissioner didn't know about him—snuffed the amusement from the momentary daydream.

***

The HTV proceeded without incident. A "food" drop at the big intersection of Lane and Bridge, and then a routine perimeter sweep where the old west bound I-196 expressway ran along the northwest edge of the neighborhood. Nothing unusual save for a bit of the 12-foot concertina-lined fencing near the Lane Avenue underpass needed a quick repair…and the half-eaten feral zombie who'd misinterpreted its ability to dig and squeeze under it. It appeared its brethren on the other side decided to take advantage of its predicament, ravaging it nearly to its ribcage. Even the undead seemed to have a limit as the thing had expired to hopefully a better place than it found in this life.

The entire time, Lettner fumed, buckled into his seat pan, arms crossed, mumbling just loud enough to be heard. Billet ignored the man, focusing on the road ahead. They neared a section of Bridge Street, which used to run uphill to the upper west side of Grand Rapids. The street went under the 196 expressway; however, no more as the west bound section of the steel and concrete span lay in a crumbled heap. Bridge Street ended here, north or south along intersecting tree-lined Valley Avenue the only routes from here.

An aged red brick building stood on the south side corner of Bridge and Valley. Without saying a word, Jake felt the Huron slow to a complete stop.

"Phelps. Mulholland. Crate detail with me." He said, as he surveyed the area. The engines died as he dropped from the open commander's hatch and back down into the transport.

"What now?" Lettner asked.

"Sit tight and shut up," Billet told him.

Phelps emerged from the driver's compartment, cutting Lettner off just as the man inhaled, presumably to breathe contemptuous fire on Billet again. Though Jake hardly believed the big, bad regent retained polite thoughts of the woman, the flame blew out and the man remained quiet.

On scheduled excursions through the UCRA, the HTV's made stops at certain homes and "ministry" installations of living inhabitants dwelling within the enclosed neighborhoods. Items not readily available to these steadfast folk were delivered right to their doorstep. Overseen by Sister Mary Mirose, the West Side Apostolate was one of the ministries the GRCC made deliveries. The six-foot-four battle-hardened nun came out to greet Jake as they dragged crates of processed Z-rations and other sundries to the front entrance of the small complex.

"Welcome. Welcome," she said cheerily, her voice coarse from years of smoking. Rolled up in the sleeves of both arms of her dirt-stained tunic, a pack of cigs attested to her addiction. The cigarette packs strained against the fabric as her thick muscled arms fought to be wrapped within those blessed folds.

The good sister assisted with bringing more crates from the rear of the Huron.

An old parochial school boy, Stokes stayed at his post atop the vehicle. He warily watched the big nun haul two crates atop her broad shoulders as the others dragged theirs through the door of the ramshackle building. Knowing how the short, easy-to-travel-the-road-to-least-redemption man could be, Billet could envision the gunner taking his fair share of ruler-rapped knuckles as he learned his religion.

The nun watched Phelps lug a crate inside the building, peering at the dark-skinned soldier's back with an approving nod that only Billet caught.

"What's on the agenda today, Captain?" Mirose said, as she and Billet stood on the sidewalk just outside the mission house.

A woman and what appeared to be her young child walked towards them, teetering side to side and dragging their feet as if heavy with drunkenness. The woman's clothing, threadbare and shredded in the front, exposed a sagging, withered teat. The patch of hair on the left side of her otherwise bald and peeling scalp, trailed away behind her. Thin brownish strands, perhaps once thick and golden when alive, flit and rolled away in the gentle breeze. Her left hand held her boy's hand, his skin a tight sheer wrap of flesh-colored drapery; his degraded muscle, bones and rotting innards showed through his paper thin skin.

Billet looked at the pair, a picture flashing in his mind of his late wife and son. These two weren't them; his son being much older when he'd been lost. Judging by the stump of a small arm in a torn, frilly sleeve in the woman's right hand—she seemed unaware and not alarmed she was missing a child—the family had been larger than his anyway.

Sister Mirose lifted a solid forearm, scarred red with bite marks. She stopped the undead woman before she walked by the building. The woman and child sniffed at both her and Billet, but showed no sign of hostility.

"Inside now. Sister Terese will see you." Mirose said, sweet as sugar, turning the woman towards the open door behind her.

The woman and boy, and bodiless small forearm, teetered and wobbled into the Apostolate.

"We can't cure their affliction, but we can treat them with a bit of decency while they are still amongst us," Sister Mary said absently scratching at a braided scar running like a red necklace from ear to ear. "Where the good Lord shows us mercy, we must show it unto others regardless of their station in life…"

More staggering civilians slowly made their way up the street. They moved not in a hungered frenzy, but a calm gait. They sniffed the air, smelling the "meat" in the crates.

"…or in unlife." She ended, stepping further out onto the sidewalk to channel the people inside the place.

"Our 'friend' inside is wondering why we're wasting time." Mulholland said, dragging another crate from the Huron, veins standing out on thin arms and forehead.

Billet looked at Sister Mary. "And when the good Lord shows you no mercy?"

He slid a twice folded piece of paper into the woman's calloused hand, glancing up at the slim radio antenna looming above them atop the building's roof. She nodded and tucked the paper beside the cigarette pack in her right sleeve.

Jake waited for Phelps to come back out, and she stepped from the murky interior almost on cue.

"You ever think of joining the sisterhood, young lady?" Mirose said with a lopsided smile, eyes falling and rising along the other woman's solid body and abundant bosom.

Loutonia cast a glance over her shoulder as she stepped past Billet. "No thanks. I like men."

Jake snorted and gave a salutatory nod to the holy sister.

"Good luck out there." Mirose said as more civilians approached, positioning themselves like a line at a soup kitchen.

There was the outer gate, the wilds outside town, roughly 30 miles to the lakeshore through independent townships and their stingy overlords, untamed undead, and homesteaders who were armed to the gill and didn't want any visitors—known or otherwise—traipsing through their backyard, especially if they got wind of his cargo…

Billet didn't need luck, he just needed to survive.

***

"Papers, Commander?" The soldier in full battle dress asked. He stood inside a dual-meshed, chain link fence, armed with a machine gun, the weapon also equipped with an M320 40mm grenade launcher. Fully padded with thick Kevlar vest and leggings, the soldiers outfit looked excessive considering the outposts quiet demeanor. The other servicemen of Grand Rapids Command Central, or "Gurks" as GRCC troops were lovingly called, were similarly heavy plated, including the lone modified Blast-Resistant Vehicle-Offroad, or BRV-O.

The soldiers manning the M-45 gate to the outer "wild" lands west of Grand Rapids were armed up and ready for action. There was nothing new about seeing a vehicle at their gate, but they perked up with the M213 Ridgerunner-class heavy vehicle gently snarling before their post.

Jake leaned over the side of the Huron and slid a packet of paperwork, his original transport orders, to the squad leader through a steel-framed "window" in the fencing. The husky lieutenant—the name Benson scrolled above his breast pocket—took the packet and started to open it. Recognizing the man, Jake suppressed a grin.

Benson tipped his helmet back and pulled the documents from the manila envelope, reading over the first several lines, focusing on the name of the massive transport vehicle, her crew, cargo, route and destination.

The side cargo door opened with a metallic screech. Lettner emerged, followed by a lanky Mulholland trying to latch onto the older man as the regent batted his hands away.

Billet groaned. "We're not out of the inner neighborhood, and definitely still in the open. Will you please get back inside?"

Transport

Lettner stopped and looked around, seeing the tall gate spanning what used to be a four-lane street under an old section of expressway. The gate before them only the first, a second, even heavier-ribbed cyclone fence, with razor wire crowning it, stood on the opposite side of the crumbled expressway. There was just enough room for the big HTV, front to back, to park between the initial gate and the larger one that opened into the Outlands.

Sliding from his stoop, Jake hit the ground and quickly walked around the transport. He held his hand on his sidearm. He looked into the wooded hills looming on either side of them.

"Come on," Jake snarled with much irritation at Lettner. "I am supposed to get you out of here in one piece." He took the stubborn man by the arm and led him back to the transport ramp.

Mulholland stood deflated and looked to expect a berating from his commander.

"We continue to make unnecessary stops." Lettner blustered like an angry child, "We don't seem to be leaving *here*."

Billet drew close to the other man's face. "Get back in the vehicle. I have Intel that says there are folks who don't want you to leave the confines of the city, and not because of your good looks and cheery character." He peered up into the tree line north of them and pointed. "You want to get sniped and sent home in a body bag, be my guest."

Lettner glanced up at the woods Billet gestured. His brow furrowed. Billet figured the man hated admitting when someone else was right. With no further reply, surprising Billet, Lettner spun on heel, pushed his way past Mulholland, and stepped back inside the confines of the Huron.

Jake shook his head, gave his gunner a nod to ease the young soldier's worries of getting his ass chewed later, and went back to Lt. Benson.

"I think I've validated part of my cargo, Lieutenant?" Jake said to Benson, who stood calmly during the whole exchange.

Benson smirked and pressed a finger to his throat mic. "Open it up."

Another trooper standing in what used to be an old bus stop shelter signaled with a thumbs up. He flipped open a metal console box. The gate before the HTV started with a jerk and rattle as it began its sidelong journey to opening. Phelps revved the twin diesels, gaining everyone's attention to stand clear as the vehicle slowly rolled into the enclosure. Even before the rear of the transport cleared the line of the fence, the gatekeeper reversed the mechanism and slid the chain link back towards the closed position.

Many others scattered about the perimeters of the inner city, the M-45 gatehouse kept the residence—the living and otherwise—safe within from the "wilds" just outside.

***

"What do you mean we are staying the night?" Lettner bellowed, his voice booming like a bouncing cannonball within the insides of the transport. "You got headlights on this thing, don't you? Or are those broke too?"

Billet wanted to clamp a hand over the man's mouth to quiet him down. Stokes lay snoring in a hammock not far from the ruckus and Phelps was in the driver's cab with the door closed. Awake, Mulholland was the only other soul who endured the yelling. His face in his hands, he looked nervously back and forth between the angry regent and his commander.

"I've been out there at night, and part of our protocol is to not do so unless absolutely necessary." Jake responded to the man. "I am not going to endanger my men."

Lettner retorted. "Unlike you, obviously, I have a schedule to keep and people waiting for my return, so if you can't make this happen any faster…"

"That's a negative. Sorry," Billet said, trying to relax his balled fists.

"Then put me in communication with your superiors," the regent barked.

"You want to make the road tougher with broadcasting your whereabouts and painting a target on your back?" Billet asked, more a statement than a question, his voice rising to match that of the frustrated regent. "You're endangering yourself, me and my crew."

Lettner opened his mouth to fire back.

"Radio communication is off limits starting now," Jake ordered.

Awake now, Loutonia peered from the cracked cab door.

Mulholland stood, rigid at attention. A bead of sweat glistened on his forehead.

Stokes stirred slightly under his coarse wool blanket, and then returned to snoring.

Lettner's face grew ten shades darker. He looked ready to go nuclear. He glared, and then said loud enough for only Billet to hear. "This is going in my report."

***

Jake leaned against a section of guard rail whose galvanized body still retained its newness considering the roadway it "guarded" lay cracked, crumpled and spotted with field grasses. The tall, dual-mesh chain link fence, encircled with razor wire at its top, continued along the section of I-196 expressway here also, lining the perimeter of the "inner city" side. Similar fencing, but electrified, spanned the Outland perimeter. From where Jake stood, he overlooked the entire west side of old town Grand Rapids—the UCRA—and the brightly-lit downtown "city proper."

The Downtown area shone like a brilliant jewel whereas the surrounding neighborhood to the west of the river stood midnight dark. A few lights glowed, small stars in a massive field of black, where a handful of rugged living, breathing folk remained within those white-lit habitations.

Inhuman screams and cries drifted to ear; the sound of the

undead who stalked the inner 'burbs. Billet wasn't a linguist like Phelps, but understood this as the means to their communication. With rotted vocal cords, the awful noise was not surprising.

Looking out into that dark neighborhood, Jake's thoughts drifted to his wife and son. His mind's eye showed an image of sunlight and warmth, a two-story home in an old industrial area of town, the emerald hue of a fresh cut lawn, and walks through a vibrant and living neighborhood. This was before they moved out of the city; moved further west towards the shores of Lake Michigan. Jenna always wanted to have a home on a chunk of old farmland, which was how she'd grown up. Immersed and fully settled and popular in the city high school, his son, Joseph, wasn't happy to leave or live so far out of town.

"If we stayed, would things have turned out different?" Billet asked aloud to the night. The dull screech and howls of the dead were his only answer, and sadly, that reply made sense.

The sound of hard-soiled boot crunching on broken pavement brought him out of his reverie. He spun him around with sidearm in hand.

"It's me, Captain," came the voice of Phelps. Her dark skin blended with the night. Only a small patch of her white undershirt shone beneath the khaki combat uniform.

"Good way to get shot." Billet said, holstering his pistol and turning back to the cityscape.

Phelps moved to a spot beside him, peering out in the same direction as he. "If it was someone else, would you have fired?"

Jake smirked. "Tempting at this point," he said. "But too close to home."

He glanced at the transport driver. Her uniform top had slid away from her jutting bosom covered in white. The coolness of the night made her stand out. He reverted his attention back to the neighborhood sprawl.

"Can't sleep?" he asked.

"Not with you and Lettner's lovers spat." She answered, trying to be jovial. She pulled the loose shirt flaps back over herself and crossed her arms over her chest.

Billet didn't respond, his thoughts far away.

"You think about them much, Phelps?" Jake asked, he looked at the few twinkles of light down in the neighborhood below. A loud bawl rose up from the darkness, followed by shrieks and gurgling howls.

"Them, sir?" Phelps responded, having an idea of what he spoke, but wanting to make sure.

"Your family."

"Always," she replied. He saw her pat her hand over her heart. "Not so much the abusive ex, he can continue to rest in pieces." She hesitated and drew a deep breath and let it out slowly. "I think about my babies. I think of them all the time."

Loutonia's ex-husband had "turned" several years ago. A drunkard and addict, the affliction, when it rolled heavy through the region, took him easily. Though no one had known, and no one generally missed his disappearance, with a glimmer of his former life's semblance, he had attacked her and her young children. The children succumbed, dying from wounds and infection while, normal for her, strong and a fighter, she pulled through to find all she had lost.

Billet was there when, at that time, his new driver had put her little ones in Oak Grove Cemetery. She visited them as often as she could with that area of town fenced off, restricted to the military only when necessary. He helped her pour the three-foot thick slabs of concrete to keep their remains below as she would not stand to see them decapitated or shot in the head. She also did not want to have to act if they clawed their way out.

"I have to wonder why we are taking the route we're taking," Loutonia said as she looked out over the city. "It's going right by your old homestead. Is that a wise thing? Some say strong emotion clouds sound judgment."

Billet turned to Phelps, gritting his teeth. "Isn't that what this is all about? Emotion? We have this monster in our midst. While the majority of his fellow constituents on the lakeshore love him, you have a scattered populace just beyond, all the way to Lansing who fear and hate him."

Jake took a breath and turned back to the city view. "That's why we were assigned this mission. To guard that monster from the folk who are ape shit to take him out..."

"I stay with you, sir, because you have always been there for me, and always been rational in the face of extreme circumstances." Loutonia interjected, not liking to see her commander seething so. "I want what's best as well, but don't want to see the mission jeopardized due to...emotion. The M-45 corridor route..."

Billet exhaled sharply, regaining control and said: "It's got to be."

Phelps opened her mouth.

"Dismissed," Jake said. He turned and looked at her. The edge leaving him, "I appreciate the concern, Lou. I do. Go get some rest. We head out of town tomorrow."

"Aye, Captain." She saluted.

Billet remained there for a moment, staring out over the night-shrouded neighborhood. A loud phlegm-filled growl made him turn and glance across the empty lanes of the highway, to the fence line cutting off the inner neighborhoods to the outer where hell and pain truly reigned. A group of hungry Ferals teetered—the wild dog zombies outside city limits; his raised voice and scent attracting them.

"Yeah, we'll see you guys tomorrow," he said towards them.

One of the them stumbled against the enclosure, throwing up a fount of sparks as it crisped itself on the electrified fence.

"Well, except for you." Billet snorted and started back towards the gate grounds and his vehicle.

CHAPTER THREE
Roadside Assistance

The morning came with the changing of the M-45 gate guard and the husks of a few electrified undead lying in the outbound lane. Fully armed and at the ready, the dozen soldiers who'd just arrived opened the dual outer gates and disposed further of the bodies with flamethrowers. The stench ruined an already less-than-exciting breakfast of dry rations and weak coffee. Stokes was the only one who kept a full appetite, going as far as asking Phelps and a green-faced Mulholland if he could finish up their MREs. Lettner sat quietly just inside the transport's rear bay, the stink seeming to have arrested his vocal cords.

"Captain, can I see you for a moment?"

Billet was surprised to see Lt. Benson hadn't rotated out with his men from the day before. The gate commander stood with dark circles under his eyes and a look not far from the hapless expressions of most undead.

"Pulling a double?" Jake asked, following the other man to the small guard shack.

"You know Renald Neilsen?" Benson said, flipping the manifest documents on his clipboard back and forth, studying the pages.

"Old Rockbottom? Yeah." Billet replied, more interested in his transport manifest he'd given the man yesterday.

"He turned last night." Benson said, rubbing at his whiskers and still peering at the manifest. "He'd been in and out of the infirmary. Took out three orderlies before they could sedate him."

Billet looked on, jaw slack in surprise.

"That's a dozen people in a little over a week by reports," Benson said. "One of the guys this morning said the townies are spooked. Thanks to your man in there." He nodded towards the big transport, "and his speeches on living within the reach of the afflicted…"

Another thing he could thank the Muskegon Councilman for, Billet thought. The guy stirred the pot wherever he could.

"Good thing I am getting him out of here then," Billet said.

"Which brings me to your traveling papers," Benson responded, throwing a wary gaze Jake's way. "According to these," the lieutenant slid out Billet's mission manifest, "you're supposed to travel on the 96-131 corridor to Spring Lake-Muskegon. I saw no other orders within that deviates you through M45."

"And you won't either," Billet returned. "Management changed our plans to divert any trouble for the regent should his home route be compromised."

Benson flipped through the paperwork.

"I am going to have to call it in to HQ just to verify." He said, stuffing the manifest back into its manila envelope.

Billet rubbed his chin. He looked at the Huron and out towards the outskirts they were about to depart. He looked at Benson with stern, dark eyes.

"You are not going to call it in," he said without emotion, staring Benson eye to eye. "The mission cannot be compromised."

"It's protocol. I call it in regardless," Benson returned. "I could jeopardize my position if I don't."

Billet watched the man move towards the radio in the steel

shack behind him.

"Stokes!" Jake yelled, stopping the gate commander in his tracks. Both men watched the squat gunner step around the transport.

"Yes, sir?" Stokes answered. He looked from Billet to Benson. Wearing his boonie hat, he tipped it in salutation at the lieutenant.

"You have anything Lt. Benson might be interested in?" Jake asked, holding a hand up, doing a victory sign, and then sliding the index finger of his other hand in the crotch of the vee. "Something that might persuade him to not jeopardize his... position?"

Stokes grinned, drove his hand into the leg pouch of his coveralls and produced a deck of dog-eared photos. He shuffled through them, chuckling at some, grimacing at others. He plucked a photo near mid-point, sour look still on his face, and handed it to Billet.

"Is this something you would also communicate to HQ?" Billet said, turning the photo over so the lieutenant could view it easily.

The blood drained from Benson's face.

Billet grinned. "Nothing has to be said. *Nothing* has to be communicated. We have an understanding?"

Benson swallowed hard. "Where'd you get that picture?"

Billet handed the picture back to his gunner. Stokes peered at it one last time, blanching.

"The sergeant here used to work surveillance on the south end of town during the '68 round up of the...citizens...over there," Billet answered. "Lots of illicit and *non-protocol* activities went on as you might recall."

"Those prostitutes might have been fine during better days," Stokes added. "But to stick it to an undead..."

"Dismissed!" Jake snapped, before Stokes carried on too far.

Though the morning crisp and cool, still pale of face, Benson's forehead bead with sweat.

Garnering some muster, Benson said with a sneer. "Safe travels, Captain."

Billet grinned all the more.

"I do need to use the radio before we head out." He said, moving towards the shack. "Personal call so, some privacy please."

Benson stood silent.

Jake stepped into the shack. A simple transmitter-receiver stood on a squat desk. He picked up the headset and microphone. The radio frequency set for communication with one of the posts near downtown, he dialed the tuner to 101.3 and pressed transmit.

"Ridge to Ranger Finder," he said twice. "Package is en route. Over."

Static replied, and then: "Message received. The road to Perdition is open."

"Understood. Will send update from Collindale when we pass through. Ridge out," Billet replied.

He returned the dial to its original setting and left the shack.

He shivered as he walked back towards the waiting transport. Exhaling deeply, he tried to exhaust the sudden onset of nervousness grappling with his system. He glanced towards the gate opening to release them into the Outlands. He'd been there before but knew this time… it would be an entirely different game.

***

"Captain, they've moved the gate again."

Climbing into the empty navigator's seat beside Phelps, Billet peered out the narrow view port at the road ahead. His fingers traced the folded map, not that he or Phelps needed it. Looking out the port, he stifled a growl of irritation. "Son of a bitch," he emitted instead.

He started to back out of the cramped driver's compartment.

Lake Michigan Drive stretched from Downtown Grand Rapids, and west to the sandy shores of Lake Michigan. Near the city, at the inner city gateway they'd left a half hour ago, where the old I-196 expressway dissected the road, M-45 officially started—though still considered *Lake Michigan Drive* until the Reganshire community enclosure. At Reganshire, roughly 17 miles to the west of the city, M-45 officially and solely became its own.

Currently, beyond the inner city gateway, heading west, houses and full out neighborhoods sprawled. However, though populated with homes on either side of the wide roadway, the area stood more vacant than the historic and catastrophic '08 Housing Market Collapse. With the viral and zombie contagion, and de-stabilization of the entire area, the Outlands were up for grabs. They were sparsely populated with roving bands of the undead and walled communities of firmly planted hangers-on. Opportunities to be had in these vacated sections, small groups of greedy low-lifes staked a claim on the blighted land and unoccupied properties.

And if these bands of surviving scum possessed the necessary fire power…

The Collindale gate wasn't an official GRCC military outpost, or one necessarily pinned on the more important maps of the region. Manned by some derelicts—reports were they were escapees from a Kalamazoo psych ward—they charged a toll for most, killed several on a whim, and kissed ass to the local armed forces. Boot licked for food and supplies.

Billet wasn't up to wasting time, nor had goods available to barter.

"Just keep moving." Jake ordered Phelps, as he started out the cab door into the bowels of the transport.

"I don't think we can fit through that span, and if I punch through it…"

The fine folks of the Collindale gate were also prone to enjoy a shoot-out with local authorities. The burned-out and twisted wreckage of an Abrams tank sat sideways in the parking lot of an old restaurant establishment. A reminder that the gate owners maintained enough ordinance to take out a big armored vehicle if they so desired.

Jake understood Phelps' hesitation to rush through it.

He stepped right into Lettner who was unbuckled and standing.

"I need some air. I already feel like I've been stuck inside a soup can for far too long," the regent said. His tone came more as a command than a statement.

"We have another check point to go through, and then Stokes can let you get a shot of skylight and whatever blows down the hatch." Jake replied, patting at Stokes' legs standing in the front gunner's hatch. "I still don't want you sticking your head up lest someone is out there waiting to put a hole in it."

Lettner growled. "I am not going to stay hold up inside this thing like an imprisoned criminal."

Jake snorted with mirth at that. He knew Lettner wasn't a stupid man, but did he think some people actually didn't view him as such. You can deal death and be the hero to some, but there are often others who were fortunate to survive and end up not sharing the same sentiment.

"Sit down, please. The Reganshire gate is not far down the road after this one," Billet said, nodding his head towards the regent's empty seat. "If you're good, I'll let you catch a breather then."

The man sat down and started to buckle in. He opened his mouth to speak, but a light seemed to flicker on in his head and his eyes grew wide.

"Wait a minute," Lettner said as he hesitated. "What route are we taking? Interstate 96 is the main route to Muskegon. That's the way we should be going…"

"I thought I told you," Jake said. "That route's been compromised. A group from the Grand Haven NSC branch is meeting us at US31, and taking you the rest of the way. News got out to the unsavory that you were heading home."

Lettner raised a brow, surprise then suspicion changing his expression.

"Another reason why I don't want you popping your head up and getting noticed. If our new route becomes compromised…" Billet left the statement unfinished, letting the other man figure it out for himself.

Turning his back on the regent, Jake squeezed the leg of Stokes getting the squat man's attention. "Keep your fingers off the trigger," he said, peering up through the open hatch, seeing the gunner's hands clenched tightly on the handles of the quad 30's.

The carrier lurched suddenly as Phelps pressed the brakes too firmly. The squeal of metal on metal sounded from outside and within. Lettner swore as he cupped his hands over his ears.

"Little tighter than I thought, Captain," Phelps called from the driver's compartment.

"Commander, you better come top side," Mulholland called from the rear gunner's hatch.

Billet moved to the secondary front hatch, climbing upon the pedestal while lifting the heavy lid. Though neither of the two gunners felt compelled to open fire on what'd gotten Mulholland's goat, Jake cautiously raised his head and upper body through the hatchway.

Considering Mulholland was in the rear section of the 30-foot carrier, it gave him a view of the entire complex. The roadway was a four-laner—two westbound and two eastbound—with a turning lane in the center. Re-positioned as they were, the outpost gates took up the entire turning lane and half the distance into each of the other lanes. It still wasn't quite the dead on 20-foot span, as the sides of the Huron pressed against the concrete-filled steel posts. Beyond the posts, blocking off the rest of the avenue, stood tall pilings of broken cement slabs, jagged rebar, and wall sections dragged from some of the defunct buildings near the street corner.

50-gallon steel drums, partially rusted, yet blackened from contents having been burned within them, jutted from the rubble. With enough blackened cartilage to keep the limb upright, a charred skeletal arm hung from one of the barrels.

"They had the best burritos." Stokes said to Billet as they peered at the dilapidated Shawmut Pub & Grub restaurant on the south side corner. The building stood directly across from them just beyond the burnt out husk of the Abrams. "Whatever they put in their recipe to spice up their ground beef..."

"I don't think I'd be too curious about what makes up their meat now." Jake said, eyes falling across crisped carcasses scattered about the restaurant's parking lot. A few of the bodies were human, and a couple other piles were so mangled he couldn't tell what they had been.

He glanced warily from the old restaurant to the defunct motorcycle dealership on the other side of the street, and back. Usually there were Mutts, residents of the outpost, happy to request a toll to pass through their gate. Fully armed with spoils from their burnt out armored trophy, they didn't need to do much enticing to have travelers pay their fee for continued passage. Not that this area was thick with Ferals or other banditry, but absence of anyone coming out to harass them made Jake's gut knot.

The transport came to a stop, wedged in between the steel post uprights of the gate.

Scanning the area one more time, Jake dropped back inside the Huron. He walked by Lettner who remained seated and glaring at him. Moving to the rear, he punched the button to lower the rear hatch.

"I can do that, Captain," Mulholland said in his earbud, though he stood practically right above him.

"I got it. Just keep your eyes peeled and gun ready."

The rear ramp crunched down on the broken pavement. Pulling his sidearm, Jake latched onto a crate of "meat" and dragged it behind him. He looked around before stepping off the ramp, though if someone wanted to plug him, this would be the most opportune time.

No shots came nor did any of the usual gate personnel. Every alarm screamed in his head, but this was one of their mission's "unlogged" stops.

"Orders, Captain?" Phelps called from the cab through Billet's earbud.

"Give me a sec and then let's move on," Billet said as Phelps triggered the rear ramp to close from her location.

Reaching the center of the restaurant parking lot, he stopped, slipped his hand into the knee pouch of his coveralls, and withdrew a crinkled note pad. Taking up an accompanying stub of pencil, he scrawled a brief note. VESPER. CARGO INTACT. CLEAR A PATH WITH REGAN. Squatting, he grabbed a small charred chunk of rubber from the destroyed tank, hefting it in his palm, assuring its weight would do the job, and sandwiched the note between the crate and chunk of tread.

Standing up, he took one last glance about the area. His eyes fell upon the crude look-out tower across the street. More niggling feelings brought his short hairs up, but still, nothing.

Phelps fired up the engines. The thunderous roar of the revved diesels and blasting snarl of the exhausts made the ground tremble and the restaurant windows rattle.

Trotting to the side of the Huron, Jake started up the rungs to the roof top, lifting a leg to clamber on top of the vehicle and back into the commander's hatch.

A sudden barrage of bullets panged off the armored hide of the HTV. He went backwards, flailing the empty air. He landed on his back, blasting the wind out of him. Machine gun fire overhead and bullets spacking all about the ground kept him from lying there. Snapping upright, he rolled to the side of the transport, ignoring the needles of pain running up his backside, thankful they weren't needles of hot lead.

"Someone's in the tower." Stokes yelled over the comm, his voice muffled, ringing hollow through the receiver. He spoke within the armored protection of the hull; Billet glad the gunner took cover versus trying to stand up to the sudden frontal assault.

"My eyes were just on it. Son-of-bitch must have woken up," Billet responded into his own throat mic.

Mulholland came over the air waves. "It's a Mutt." He said, hesitating for a heartbeat. "But he doesn't look so good."

Billet didn't have to ask Mulholland what he meant by that last statement.

Catching movement from within the old restaurant, he scrambled for cover underneath the Huron's belly a second before the ground where he'd just lain plumed with a fresh barrage of gun fire. He was surprised he hadn't been hit as the Mutt's were all known and proven marksmen. But as the shooters swayed through the open restaurant front and side doorways, he understood why.

"Mutt in the tower has Turned," came Phelps from within the vehicle, using a cab side port for viewing the situation.

Jake peered between the gap of the massive dualies he laid behind. The three men and two women moving towards the Huron held their weapons firmly in hand, firing though unfocused. He could see their blank gazes, their loose lower jaws hanging open. Their flesh a gray hue. The lead foot soldier had a fresh chunk missing from his neck. He was drenched from shoulder to waist in his own blood.

The freshly-turned were the most dangerous of all. They retained just enough of their fading life's memory and skill to put a person in a quick pickle if not paying attention.

Billet pulled himself tighter against one of the big wheels as the undead Mutts raked his side of the transport with gun fire. He caught movement on the roof of the restaurant between the plumes of smoke and kicked-up debris, pulling his head back behind the big tires after another hurried peek.

"Shit," he said into the throat mic. "RPG on the roof! RPG on the roof!"

The Mutts were vicious, even in unlife. The ground troops and guy in the tower held them down, while their guy with the grenade launcher set up for the kill.

"Phelps, get movin'...*now*!" Billet howled. "Stokes cover Mulholland. Mulholland..."

Mulholland finished Jake's sentence: "I'm on him, Captain."

"Auto-cannon, sir?" Stokes said over the comm, Billet surprised he was asking.

The 40mm grenade launcher would return volley at the Mutt on the roof. If Stokes missed it was one literal round lost, and the RPG-toting Mutt's turn to serve. And the Mutt had a bigger target than Stokes.

And the sergeant wasn't well known for his precision.

"Negative. Emergency use only," Billet responded. "Spray 'em with lead."

Pistol in hand, Jake fired without aim, and rolled to the center point of the Huron's belly. He'd rather catch a bullet than get crushed beneath the massive rear tracks. Just below the cab section, a tow ring jut from the center of the vehicle's undercarriage. He grasped the ring as the transport shuddered and started to move forward. The squeal of metal on metal mixed with the loud burp of gunfire.

"This is gonna ruin my new paint job," Phelps quipped.

Billet swore as he tried to angle himself so his hard leather sidearm holster rode between him and the pavement. He didn't want to lose his pistol, yet his hand and arm attached to the tow ring threatened to come out of socket.

The transport cleared the gate.

The undead Mutts made their way into the street still firing.

"Where are you, Commander?" Mulholland called.

"Underneath you." Billet said, stifling a cough from the road dust kicked up around him. "Nail the RPG."

The transport lurched to a halt, the jerking motion made Jake's arm ache worse.

"The crate, or the gun?" Mulholland replied.

"I got the crate," Stokes responded over the bark of his 30's.

The belly hatch didn't open so Billet crawled out from under the vehicle. He looked to the Mutt with the RPG. Though the shooter's head leaned lazily to one side, he leveled the weapon towards the HTV. Sharp pain shot through his chest as Jake raised his pistol to take a shot. He grit his teeth, suspecting a bruised or broken rib. It took all his effort to raise the gun shoulder level, not high enough to shoot at the RPG bearer.

"Mulho..."

The lone .30-Cal popped once as the young gunner squeezed off a single round. The Mutt's head disappeared, his arms dropping but not before the dying trigger finger fired the rocket. The weapon angled down. The explosive round slapped into the restaurant roof. The Mutt disappeared in a violent roar of yellow-orange flame. A boiling cloud propelled black smoke, splintered timber and hot, twisted metal into the air. The Mutts on the ground staggered sideways, some fell, as the concussion of the close quarter blast bowled them over.

Immediate threat down, Mulholland and Stokes opened up on the remaining outpost folk. The Mutt zomb in the tower was first to be shred under a barrage of machine gun fire.

On his feet, Billet awkwardly climbed the rungs to the roof of the transport. "Go, go, go!" He shouted into his throat mic.

A hand thrust in his face. He looked up to see Lettner sprawled low on the rooftop, offering assistance.

"I'll help you up," Lettner said, flinching as Stokes guns barked behind him.

Billet looked at him incredulously, as if the man were offering the zombie contagion himself.

The transport shuddered to a start again, nearly shaking Jake from his perch. He holstered his pistol and threw his hand up, clasping the regent. Making the rooftop, he clambered back down into the bowels of the vehicle behind Lettner as the burp of the guns topside slowed their blasting.

"I thought I told you to keep your head down?" Jake said to Lettner. His heart pounded in his chest, making his ribcage ache with every drumming beat. He felt suddenly like sitting down.

Lettner staggered as the Huron bucked, rolling over something. "Seemed you were in a tight spot, and everyone else was busy." He said, sitting down and fumbling with the five-point harness.

Billet didn't have the energy to rag on the man. He had to admit he might have been hanging out there waiting for a stray bullet if the man hadn't stuck his neck out. Still, if the regent got hit and killed...

The transport grumbled.

"Must've hit a coolant line. I'm starting to run hot, commander," Phelps said.

Jake groaned.

"You feed 'em, Stokes?" Jake said, glancing up at the gunners stand, referring to the crate of processed brain meat he'd left outside. His thoughts were more on the wasted message atop the crate.

Mulholland broke in, throwing a verbal jab at his gunner companion up front. "Drained the munitions..."

"Yeah, I got it." Stokes snarled with irritation at Mulholland's prodding. "I still have about fifty rounds left." His voice trailed away. "Asshole."

"Enough." Billet said, taking a seat across from Lettner who sat silently staring at him. "Take inventory of what we used and have left. We'll make a pit stop at the Reganshire communal and make any necessary repairs, and check for any further exterior damage."

"Reganshire? Silas Regan? The old Standale Outpost?" Lettner perked up.

"That's the place."

Jake's gut churned knowing what harried Lettner.

A huge adversary of Lettner and the North Shore Coalition, Silas Regan was a violent, unpredictable leader of the large village west of Grand Rapids. Barred from attending the Grand Rapids meeting with the Muskegon High Councilman; security and fear of some form of retaliatory action had been high. Regan begrudgingly did business with the big city yet was well known for paying lowly killers to sneak into high places to off folk he felt little fondness for. He was no less ruthless than Lettner, except the Muskegon man held vast more power, properties and resources, thus an intense envy and resultant hatred.

Billet's plans were to cruise by the village and outpost formerly known as Standale without too much interaction with the populace, especially old man Regan.

"You *will* stay on the down low when we make our stop," Jake said, buckling himself into his seat pan with a bit more bravado than needed. "We might both lose our heads if you don't."

Lettner nodded, crossing his arms over his broad chest, and lowered his head.

Jake couldn't tell if the regent prayed or simply meditated on more peaceful thoughts to quell any anxieties. Jake was nervous; nervous as hell. The stop and message at the now-destroyed Collindale OP was supposed to be forwarded to their undercover colleague on the inside of Reganshire to make sure they rolled through without question. The communiqué lost meant his contact wouldn't know they were en route.

Like the Mutt's, the community at Reganshire enjoyed bartering with force if you had something they wanted. And unlike the dozen or so who *had* been part of the Collindale Outpost, Reganshire was a good-sized village. Last census, the old western suburb of Grand Rapids—the last before you truly headed out into the boondocks—totaled nearly a thousand living souls and a small army of their self-trained "junkyard zombies;" semi-doped Ferals on leashes.

Jake secured the last clasp as Mulholland and Stokes rummaged about the insides of the transport, counting their remaining ammunition cases. He lowered his head and closed his eyes.

It was his turn to pray.

CHAPTER FOUR
Civilization's End

They rolled through the rubble which once was the greater village of Standale. It had been a landscape of quaint homes and commercial buildings; just like many of the suburbs around Grand Rapids proper. Further west, similar to Standale, the VSU communal and Allendale existed in the Outlands. However, the place was now called Reganshire, and it stood out as a bit more...unique.

Billet stood in the commander's hatch as the Huron growled slowly along the vacant roadway. His gaze roamed across the debris-strewn lots and old residential avenues. He'd seen acres of woodland stripped less bare than what used to be the streets and homes of this once bustling and vibrant community. A massive piece of property stood on the southwestern edge of the village. Once a major supermarket with several smaller businesses peppered around it, the huge lot became the heart of the area when the virus and undead came full on. The community scrounged every piece of useable material, destroying neighboring homes and buildings to erect and fortify the barbed-wire and rubble-lined enclosure which Old Man Regan now ruled. So barren and broken was the rest of the former small town, someone might assume the place had been used for a bombing run.

Silas Regan and his folk were thorough, which gave Jake a sinking feeling. It would be hell for the transport to get by with Lettner and not end up getting all their heads on a pike.

"Shitty goddamn luck," he swore under his breath again regarding the Collindale Outpost episode. Even without engine trouble, without the updated ETA message getting to his guy on the inside, Jake knew they would have to stop. He had a better chance at French kissing a Feral zomb than he would at talking his vehicle and crew through Reganshire's armed check points without getting stopped and thoroughly searched.

"We're royally gonna be fucked," he said to himself.

***

The perimeter fencing rose fifteen feet towards the overcast sky. Behind it, a wall of cement blocks formed an additional barricade and protection for the line of closet-sized guardhouses and machine gun bunkers. Ingeniously designed against small arms and explosives use, the thick corrugated sheet metal was angled just enough to deflect such things from their people and bunkers.

Jake could appreciate their resourcefulness, but felt no comfort inside the enclosure at the moment.

"You must be carrying some sort of orders or travel manifest." A burly man in military fatigues demanded, looking up at Billet. The giant of a soldier had no neck and looked as if he could bench press his whole crew bundled together.

Jake stood in the commander's cupola, paperwork in hand. Routine.

In the gunner's cupola across from him, Stokes stood jittery with fury knuckles wrapped inside the trigger guards. "At ease, soldier, at ease," Jake said out of the corner of his mouth.

"Paperwork's right here," Jake replied to the big soldier, leaning over the side of the vehicle as the man reached up for the packet. "And you are…" He pinched the packet so the other could not simply pluck it away.

"Lucius LaRouge, commander of Reganshire North gate." The big man said with a southern drawl almost as thick as Mulholland's. He thrust out his chest, and then relaxed as he took the packet.

Lucius, the Red. Nice, Jake thought. He peered at Lucius and the smaller, normal-sized men gathered round him, all with rifles and pistols at the ready. There was some military-issued hardware in the group. Jake took a glance across the compound. Folks with "blood hounds," captured Ferals, walked the grounds. The creatures sported shock collars and were "leashed" on the end of guide poles. He caught sight of a few ZiTs, or ZT's—zombie troopers—being corralled away from his view.

Using undead military personnel was highly illegal.

"You seem to be a little off course, Captain." Lucius said looking up from the documents. A dangerous smirk appeared under the Cro-Magnon ledge of the big man's jutting brow.

Military convoys and patrols weren't unknown outside Grand Rapids. When need arose, the GRCC often went to outlying towns, villages and outposts delivering goods that were essential to survival. Since the big city still produced and monopolized many of these goods, distribution runs were common. However, this didn't mean the smaller towns and villages showed appreciation of their larger, assisting city as sometimes delivered goods, vehicles and associated personnel would disappear—especially if the paperwork happened to get misplaced regarding goods, vehicle and personnel. If a province outside city central couldn't be fingered for illicit activities, the city central authorizing body and her military group typically stayed put.

The look on the gate commander's face informed Billet the man might be thinking this could be his opportunity.

"We're on a distribution run. It's not supposed to be broadcast because of the load of meat we're carrying," Jake said without pause.

He had rehearsed many scenarios and many reasons regarding the route he took. Even the end result, when Lettner was delivered back into the hands of his "adoring" constituents; each route could send Jake and his crew straight to Hell. It was why he replied so confidently. "If we took the route on the paperwork…"

He didn't have to finish. Lucius was nodding. The big man had obviously lived in the Outlands for a while.

The smirk remained. "How much you carryin'?"

Billet saw some of the other folk on the ground shift uncomfortably. Grips tightened on pistol and rifle stocks.

"Shit, man. They're gonna attack us," Stokes mumbled.

Jake put his hand up to halt the tense gunner. A bead of cold sweat rolled down the side of his face.

"Listen, we had a slight altercation at the Collindale Outpost. Got a shot up coolant line that needs replacing or we're not gonna complete our run." Jake expected a bullet to perforate his skull. "You can check our cargo. We can barter a bit if need be."

LaRouge's grin grew, nearly ear to ear. "Yeah. Barter," he chuckled as if it had been a punch line to a joke.

"I'll open the rear doors," Billet said, putting his hands up in a sign of surrender, as if that might appease the big gorilla and his gun-toting throng.

As he and Stokes lowered themselves from the hatches into the bowels of the transport, a symphony of safety's clicked off and a few shotguns being racked followed them.

Phelps stood halfway out of the driver's compartment. Lettner was partially unbuckled from his harness, and Mulholland stood from his seat pan holding his gut.

"Our friends are coming inside for inspection to see what can be bartered for repairs," Billet said as he stepped down onto the metal walkway. "I want Lettner and you…" he said to Loutonia, "…in the cab with doors closed. There is no need for them to poke their snouts in there."

Loutonia wrinkled her nose like she'd just got a whiff of shit. She missed the look of lust from Lettner's roving eyes.

Jake snagged a hooded flak jacket hanging above one of the empty interior fold-downs. He tossed it to Lettner. It smelled musty and had a slight layer of dust on the shoulder sections. The regent wrinkled his nose as he took it and held it out before him.

"Put that on. Hood up." Billet told Lettner as the regent, with much trepidation, pulled on the flak jacket. "Give him access to the sidearm box." Jake finished, looking to Phelps again.

Stokes stood close by, tapping the toe of his boot on the steel grating. The squat trooper was spoiling for a fight, and Billet knew it. A whirling dervish of destruction was nice to have on your side, but not so good when times called for controlled calm.

The big rear hatch gonged under heavy fists. LaRouge's muffled voice came from the other side, anxious, it sounded, for the vehicle to open its doors.

"You will keep your composure," Billet said to Stokes. "And your fingers off any triggers unless I tell you."

Stokes nodded, understanding, but his foot continued to tap nervously on the grating.

Jake turned to find Mulholland walking towards the rear of the vehicle.

"Where ya going, Corporal?"

"To the head, sir."

"We're in deep shit, and you're about to make more?"

"I've been holding it since Collindale, sir," Mulholland replied. His stomach grumbled loud enough for everyone to hear. He grimaced and stepped closer to the closet-sized water closet.

With nerves and guts twisted tight, Billet wrestled to maintain his own intestinal fortitude.

"Get it done and get back out here, so our guests don't decide to investigate and find you in a compromising position."

Mulholland salute, even as his belly continued to growl. He

did a quick skip-hop to the interior lavatory and closed the door behind him.

"Awright, folks, let's get moving," Jake said as the rear hatch bonged with more fists.

As he brushed by Lettner, who had venom in his eyes, the regent opened his mouth to speak.

"Yeah, yeah. This'll go on *your* report." Jake waved him on as the regent followed Loutonia into the drivers cab, shutting the door behind them.

"Don't know why we simply don't turn over that uppity baby-killin' son of a bitch to these clowns." Stokes snarled, nodding his head towards the banging rear hatchway. "I wouldn't lose any sleep over it, I can tell you that."

"I've been thinking," Stokes continued. Checking his sidearm, Jake would have chuckled at the statement if the gunner's prior words hadn't got his own gears grinding. "I've been thinking," he repeated. "Aren't we going straight through your old stomping grounds? You, the wife and boy still lived out there when Lettner sanctioned that surprise cleansing of some lake shore properties. Was only supposed to affect the undead wandering about the area."

Stokes turned to check his own sidearm, still talking, "I don't know how you do it, Captain. I don't know how you can keep yourself in check when you are towing the piece of crap responsible for snuffing your own family. An accident? *Shhh*-it. He took out half his North Shore Coalition opposition buddies who were conveniently touring the area at the time."

For a brief moment, Jake could hear the thunder of the bio-bombs pounding the farms, woodlands and homes of West Olive Township. He hadn't been there, at home, at the time. He'd found out via all the remaining television stations aired the news post-strike. Across state, in Lansing for training, he didn't understand why his wife hadn't picked up the phone. As the terrible truth broke, the reason why she didn't answer struck him like an exploding grenade.

Transport

He hadn't been there when his wife and teenage son died, and it'd torn a chunk out of him bigger than any zombie bite ever could. No one was allowed into West Olive until the cloying yellow dust fully dissipated. By the time relatives could get to their loved ones, the bio-agent had completely done its job reducing muscle, organs and soft tissue into a gooey paste. Fear and rage were subdued quickly by the resulting Kinship Treaty. Lettner and his supporting NSC affiliates could not "dust for zombies" or pursue eradication outside their own properties without corresponding state-side permission.

The thundering of the fists and a shotgun blast against the side of the hull brought Billet back to the present. The rage still burned hot, and his gunner's words tweezed with razor sharpness against his already sensitive nerves.

It took every ounce of Jake's reserve to speak through grit teeth, "Let's open the door and show our guests in."

***

Stokes looked at Billet angrily as they stood with their hands up.

"Nice vehicle you got here, Captain," Lucius LaRouge said as he and a gang of his raggedly-dressed men rummaged through the interior of the transport.

Four of the group held Billet and Stokes at gunpoint while the others opened anything not locked down; Jake was sure they'd want keys and combinations next.

A Reganshire man stepped up and opened a large rolling toolkit strapped to one of the hull's vertical ribs. He one-handed a rifle so old and in disrepair Jake could envision it blowing up in the man's face the moment he *thought* about touching the trigger. Tucking as many tools away as possible until they threatened to pull down his already sagging trousers, the man looked at Billet through the one eye not covered by a patch, and smiled triumphantly. Even in the dimly lit interior, his mouthful of gold teeth gleamed.

Jake went to open his mouth before Lucius, watching the

activity, cut in: "He's our lead mechanic. He'll be helping you fix your vehicle. The tools will be payment for *his* services."

"My driver will want to assist in the repair." Billet shrugged and watched the shifty mechanic depart.

LaRouge nodded, peering up and down the interior of the HTV. "Yes, yes. This is a very nice rig, Captain. Clean. Roomy. Would make a great scavenger vehicle," the big man said, rubbing a thick index finger against his chin.

Jake wasn't so concerned about the vehicle being commandeered compared to what they would do to him and his crew. Silas Regan added very few people to his fold and used the extra as fodder for a sporting event chillingly referred to as "The Zombie Dash." Participants usually got the worst end of the "race."

"Considering our course isn't on the map, Command knows exactly where we are supposed to be," Billet said as he watched a stranger open his personal locker. A grimey faced boy darted in between the man's legs, and started rummaging through it. A couple of pit-stained but clean, white t-shirts left the vehicle under the boy's arm.

"This is one of the few big transports the city has," Jake continued as Lucius moved towards the front of the Huron. "I would think they wouldn't be happy with losing it...considering I know Mr. Regan is an esteemed council member."

It was bullshit, but...

Lucius spun on his heels.

Billet hadn't seen it on his person initially, but the big man unholstered a big tiger-striped Desert Eagle. Jake's eyes grew wide. Only one man brandished such an ornate sidearm, and he and his entire platoon had been lost during a skirmish in nearby Grandville over a year ago.

"Are you threatening me...*Captain?*" LaRouge snarled, pressing the big pistol barrel to Billet's forehead.

The men around him tensed. Jake saw fingers flex around

triggers. More disturbed by the idiots ready to open fire inside an enclosed steel drum, he paid little attention to the main idiot threatening to put a bullet in his brain.

A sudden muffled shout and something hitting the bulkhead inside the drivers cab caused the big Reganite to flinch. The gun barrel jammed into Billet's flesh. It would leave an imprint, less so than the imprint of a lead slug.

Everyone turned when the interior cab door squealed open. Loutonia leaned out, ready to step into the main chamber of the Huron, and stopped mid-stride as she noticed the crowd.

"Excuse me, gentlemen," she said, glancing about momentarily until she met Jake's gaze. Her brown eyes gleamed with apology. She rubbed her bloodied elbow as she spoke. "Captain," she hesitated, chewing her lip, "Navigator Parsons got grabby, and," more hesitation, "there was a slight altercation between us."

Billet noticed Stokes' look of surprise upon the name of the ex-crew member until a few years ago. Private Nathaniel Parsons had been killed in action during a mission inside the UCRA. It had been a bitter pill for Jake to swallow, any of his crew viewed as family. He was slightly surprised Loutonia used the name, however it fit in the situation. He couldn't chide her for her quick thinking.

Still, Jake grew worried from the sorry expression on his driver's face. She punched with the force of a sledgehammer. He hadn't experienced it firsthand, but on multiple occasions had stood by as she laid low many a testosterone frenzied man or three with those steel coiled muscles.

Lucius let him squeeze by to peek inside the cramped cab.

"You didn't...kill him, did you?" He noticed Lettner's chest rising and falling even as Phelps answered, he had only been slugged into unconsciousness.

Behind Billet, he could hear the astonished gasps and mumblings of the Reganshire men, their lewd thoughts seeping out through their mouths. "Ain't seen airbags like that in a while." "How do I enlist?" Were some of the comments that float to his ears.

If Loutonia heard them, she paid no heed.

LaRouge and a dirty, bald headed grunt peered into the cab, eyes falling on the big black female driver before surveying the rest of the interior. The hood of the flak jacket fell just over the regent's forehead down to the bridge of his nose. A splatter of blood spread across the left side of his mouth from a split lip, and a rivulet flowed down around his lower jaw, a crimson worm that weaved and then dropped onto the front of his vest.

"Your...navigator...looks familiar," the bald Reganshire man said as he leaned into the cab space. He lifted a hand towards Lettner's hood.

Billet tensed.

Shit was about to hit the fan. Hard.

There came activity towards the rear of the Huron. Guns suddenly swung about and took fresh aim as, squealing on dry hinges, the lavatory door swung open. Weapons drooped and sour looks spread across the faces of the gun-wielders.

Like a school boy caught slipping out of the booth from his first peep show, Mulholland donned an innocent expression. His cheeks grew rosy as he stepped into the backed-up throng. "Sorry 'bout that, fellas," he said, raising his hands and fighting back a grin.

The men looked at him, avoiding him like a leper until he shut the door to the head.

"Well, kick my goat and call me Billy," Lucius roared upon sight of Mulholland. He pushed his way through the gun-toting crowd towards the lanky gunner.

The bald man started to follow, and Billet stepped between him and the open cab door. Attention, thankfully, shifted from their unconscious occupant.

Mulholland's eyes lit up and a toothy smile spread across his mug, while the others within his proximity still frowned.

"Lucius LaFleur?" he howled.

Lucius's men stared up at him as he stopped before the gunner.

The huge gate commander threw his arms around Mulholland, a mighty oak entangling itself about a tall, lean sapling. The gunner returned the greeting. They hugged and patted each other's back, speaking excitedly like long lost brothers. Jake could hardly understand their words as both spoke, their drawl layering over the others into an indecipherable jumble until they slowed down.

"Captain, I'd like you to meet an old childhood friend," Mulholland said as the mountain and the tall twig separated. "And a buddy of mine, Lucius LaFleur. We both served down in the Fort McClellan National Guard unit in Alabama."

"I know where Fort McClellan is," Jake responded, peering warily at Lucius, or whatever his name was.

"Changed your name and everything," Mulholland said looking at the man's name patch on his uniform. "I thought I heard a familiar voice out there."

The gate commander seemed to deflate a bit, and said in a lower voice. "Didn't feel my last name would get me much, so I went with something a bit different."

"Why don't we take this outside," Billet said, not keen with all the live weapons and twitchy trigger fingers within their confined space. And the air hung stagnant still from Mulholland's restroom ruination.

Everyone agreed without hesitation.

Billet growled none too happy as the group wandered back out of the Huron's interior. Several men had dragged off crates of meat and a small footlocker full of first aid equipment. Frustrating as hell, but not surprising, and, so far, he still had his head on his shoulders.

***

Jake sat in an old rickety folding chair a few yards from the transport, casually surveying his surroundings

Stokes leaned against the Huron, thick arms folded across his broad chest. He looked miserable, yearning for nothing more than to throw a fist into the face of the next person who came close to the vehicle.

Phelps and Patch—the one-eyed, gold-toothed Reganshire mechanic—were ratcheting and clanking about in the engine compartment.

Mulholland had gone off with his behemoth of a friend an hour ago. They hadn't ventured far, moving to an old coffee shop converted into guard quarters for the north side of the compound. The small square building housed LaFleur—*"The Flower"* yeah, that *was* funny Billet thought in hindsight—and his small retinue of gate guardsmen. He could see the small crowd still gathered around the two friends who were sharing tales of the "old days." Jake told Mulholland not to go far, reasoning the repair on the vehicle wouldn't take long and, unsaid, still didn't trust LaFleur or any of the Reganites.

Mulholland had mentioned he and Lucius served in the Alabama National Guard before things had gotten bad down there. The South was a mess with the zombie affliction, no new news to Billet. He had met more recruits and more families who'd become residents of Michigan after hasty pilgrimage out of the heavily infested Southern states.

Across the compound, Billet saw two people hurry another set of zombie troopers across the open field that used to be the supermarket parking lot. They could see the big military transport sitting there, and knew by now there were Gurk soldiers in their midst. He shook his head. Silas Regan surely realized he flirt with disaster in keeping and flaunting undead soldiers on his property.

If I was a good soldier, Jake quipped to himself, I'd be calling this in the moment we got out of here.

He looked back at the HTV, knowing what was to become of the *contents* within.

"You decided to stop without calling or sending a message?"

Billet peered up at the unexpected speaker standing beside him. A man in a moth eaten gray wool cap and faded military jacket with faded jeans stood over him, close enough that his whisper of a question was only heard by Jake. Standing a few feet away, the other Reganshire guards did not hear the new arrival.

Jake knew the man the moment he looked into the scar ravaged face.

"Wasn't planning on you missing the call, and wasn't planning on stopping."

One of the nearby guards turned and looked at them. The new companion quickly offered Jake a cigarette, which he took but did not light, and peered down at the tip of his own boots. The guard nodded at the man beside Billet and returned to what he was doing.

Jake proceeded in telling the man about the issue at the Collindale Outpost that disrupted his opportunity to get a message to him.

"Things are getting more crazy out there," the other man said, absently rubbing a long, red scar that ran the length of his cheek.

Billet nodded.

"Not hearing word of your whereabouts, for a while there, until I saw your rig pull in, I thought maybe you changed your mind on the whole thing."

Jake shook his head. "No. Still a go. Main cargo is nursing a dented skull and bruised ego after trying to manhandle Phelps."

The other snorted with mirth, but let it blow out short. "You're taking a big chance on your career, your rig and crew, my friend. And for what, the money? Revenge?"

"Both." Jake answered. "Gonna need the cash to either bail me out of the brig, or for a new life and identity somewhere.

"There's only one of my crew who knows what is going down. My gunners think we're just on a highly covert stop-n-drop mission.

They'll know the skinny at mission's end, and hopefully not bust my balls too hard over it."

The other man couldn't find anything else to say.

"What's going on here, Vesp? Anything interesting?" Billet asked to change the subject. He looked at the cigarette and handed it back to the man.

William "Vesper" Aikens worked undercover for the GRCC intelligence group. He and Billet had gone through training together at Fort Custer, and gone into separate fields. Operatives like Vesper slid into common roles within other growing villages and towns, Aikens becoming part of the Reganshire community. No one questioned other military folk joining communities outside of Grand Rapids. In fact, almost all the smaller communities were glad to acquire someone with such a background.

Aikens. Mulholland. LaFleur.

A small world for sure.

Aikens pulled a lighter from his pocket and lit up. He closed his eyes and took a long drag, exhaling slowly, savoring the entire action.

"Don't know how much you've heard. I haven't seen old man Silas much lately, but he's got his folk working on their own processing plants, got some places gone up a bit south of here," the man said, watching the cigarette smoke dissipate before taking another drag. "They want to be totally self-sustainable by next year."

That didn't surprise Billet. A lot of communities, if large enough, were going the same way rather than rely on Grand Rapids completely.

"They have a textile mill and a small meat processing plant. A larger meat plant is in the works."

Billet said with an amused grunt, "That'll make the big politicos and the fat cats who own G.R.'s factories unhappy."

Aikens nodded in agreement.

"I see they've been taking on some ZiTs," Jake said watching another group of Reganites hustle a pair of soldiers across the compound.

Aikens glanced in the direction Billet peered. "Yeah, they ain't too smart about that," he took another drag from the cigarette. "Old man Regan isn't part of that scene though."

Billet glanced at Aikens with a raised brow.

"It's your old girlfriend," Aikens said, suddenly straightening. He dropped the cigarette on the ground and quickly ground it out.

Billet rubbed his face with his hands. Yet another reason why he wanted to avoid Reganshire but roll on through: Rebecca Regan, an old high school acquaintance. In school (that seemed another planet ago) she had always been after him. A few grades ahead of her, she liked the idea of having an older beau and her target was him. A spoiled little bitch then, it only got worse when he told her no. She ruined every relationship he pursued in school by threatening the poor girls he dated. Luckily, he had met his wife after those crazy school days.

"That was over twenty years ago," Billet waved the other man off, "They will have the GRCC down on them in a heartbeat if the city authorities catch wind of their activities using military personnel." Billet said, as he recalled a particular high school dance where Rebecca threatened him and his date with a pointy stiletto-heeled shoe in hand. She had actually tried to stab him with it. Punching a girl wasn't his style, but it happened that once. It got him thrown out of the dance and beaten bloody after school by the bitch's older brother and his cronies.

"Do they know what they are getting themselves into?"

Aikens cleared his throat and started to back away from him.

"Perhaps you can ask her yourself," he said, his voice suddenly fading.

Jake turned as a willowy blond with purpose in her long-legged strides, escorted by a dozen armed men, walked his way.

"Seize that man, and prep the gallows." Rebecca Regan

screeched, pointing an accusing finger at him. "He didn't dance with me before, maybe he will dance with me now."

CHAPTER FIVE
A Damsel Non-Distressed

The hazy sunlight grew back into his momentary blackened vision as Billet rose up from hands and knees. His jaw throbbed, but seemed still attached. He tasted blood as his tongue probed his battered gum line, he'd check for loose teeth later. He wanted to tell the woman she hit like a girl, but he expected it would be asking to be walloped again. And the statement was far, far from the truth.

"You've been eating your Wheaties," Jake said gaining his feet. The world teetered for a second then righted itself.

"How dare you come uninvited into my home," Rebecca Regan hissed.

She threw a roundhouse punch at him again. Not caught off guard as he'd been a second ago, he easily leaned away to avoid the blow.

He caught the slight breeze following her strike. The strong smell of tar assaulted his nostrils as something wet hit his face. Regaining his composure, he wiped the moist spot from his stubble-rough cheek, brushing, surprisingly, a wriggling maggot from himself.

Her guards tensed, ready to pounce. Stokes stood behind the

group, staring at the woman as if in a trance.

Billet looked at Rebecca's right arm, the one swung at him. She wore dark blue coveralls cinched tightly at the waist. He recalled she had always been slender, with a delicate, yet defined figure. A foot shorter than his six-foot stature, she still possessed legs that went up to her neck. Admittedly she had been a hot little number in school, though her possessive, explosive, and almost psychotic nature (and the fact he had no interest in her) kept him away.

Looking upon her now, he couldn't say the years had been bad to her, yet there was a definite change, at least in appearance, more unsettling than alluring. Her long golden hair now a thinner, snow white, the gossamer strands waved with the breath of a phantom breeze. Her skin appeared as discolored as her hair, in fact, if her flesh were a tad darker shade of gray she might be mistaken for a statue. He refrained from telling her she should enjoy more sunlight.

The Reganshire woman noticed Billet's gaze upon her features, taking it as a sign of interest. Her venomous expression flipped to a warm smile under a batting of long, colorless eyelashes. She stepped closer to him, and he looked into eyes that were once glimmering cerulean globes. The dull gray orbs now matched the hue of her skin.

"It's been a long time, Jakesy." Rebecca cooed, her pale eyes dropping to his lips.

Billet stepped back. Flies circled his head and the stink of pitch poked at his nostrils. The sleeve of her right arm, rolled back a tad, revealed a thick wrap of surgical bandages. A spot of yellowish-red pus seeped through the gauze. A fly landed, probed and launched off the spot when she found his gaze and quickly pulled down her shirt sleeve.

"We've been by before, dropping off goods this place bought from Grand Rapids," Jake answered. He watched others take notice of their leader's daughter out and about, and moved towards them. Mulholland and his buddy LaFleur walked up with the gathering throng. "I've seen your father once or twice when he's visited the city. Where's he off to today?"

Rebecca looked him up and down, trying to determine what information she should feed him. If she were anything like her father, she would talk with much pride in the family's endeavors and future plans. From what Aikens told him, she had a lot to blab about. The processing plants didn't bother him. Though he wasn't privy to the information until he'd heard it from his inside guy, he was fairly certain the higher ups back at Central likely knew Reganshire's activities.

"He'll be back shortly," Rebecca said, hesitating, eyes gazing over her retinue as if she waited for someone to correct her. "He's just checking some of our…expansions…south of here."

"I've heard you are working on your own industry here," Billet replied.

"Does the big city council find issue with that? Have you come here to spy on us?" she said, her gaze back upon him, her tone laced with less suspicion and more lascivious as she continued to eye him.

"Not at all," said Billet, fighting back a shiver. "As hopefully your North Gate Commander will inform you, we were on a distribution run when we ran into a bit of opposition and stopped for some engine repair."

Jake looked at the towering LaFleur. The Reganshire woman looked at the big man and he seemed to shrink under her gaze even as he nodded his confirmation.

Rebecca scrutinized the HTV behind Billet. Already the crates removed from the vehicle had been brought to smaller sheds peppering the compound.

"We thank you for your contributions," Rebecca said with a mocking bow.

As she bowed, she extended her left hand as if waiting for Billet to take it and kiss it. The action made the arm sleeve slide back to her elbow. A series of pin holes dotted her forearm weeping yellowish pus. As she bent, her fine white locks shifted forward. When she stood straight again, a few curling wisps fell to the ground at her feet.

Billet recoiled at the sight, his eyes locked on her track-marked arm. He had known her as a pristine kid, spoiled by her father. Even considering he thought her a crazy bitch, he could not imagine she was a junkie. But the telltale signs were a bright flashing marquee, those weeping marks on that light ashen flesh. Obviously whatever she was shooting into her body was rotting her from the inside out.

Another realization hit him as he saw a fresh group of Reganites usher a pair of ZT's across the compound towards a lone outbuilding. Bile rose in his throat and he fought it down even as he stifled an outward shiver.

"Something wrong, my love?" She said in a sickly sweet tone that made his nausea escalate.

A scuffle near the Huron drew their attention. Patch, the Reganshire one-eyed mechanic, stumbled from the engine hatch. Holding his face, he ran down the roadway from the big rig towards the converted supermarket building. He looked back as if expecting pursuit; pain and fear in his eye.

Phelps slid from the engine hatch. She watched the man flee, straightening her uniform. She looked at the crowd staring her way, waved, grimaced and sucked at her knuckles.

"Almost done here, Captain" The woman called, looking to Billet. She smiled weakly and backed into the hatchway, disappearing into the cramped engine compartment.

Stokes hadn't paid the event a notice, his eyes locked on Rebecca.

The distraction allowed Jake's senses to return. He looked at the Regan woman with fresh resolve. Rebecca's gaze locked with his and a sly grin upturned one corner of her mouth; she knew what he suspected and her look was one of uncaring knowledge of such.

Transport

Disgust and anger drew him up, and he took a step towards the woman. She batted her eyelashes and cocked a hip as if trying to pose alluringly. He reached to throttle her but her guards snapped to attention, leveling their weapons in his direction.

Jake placed his hands softly on her bony shoulders.

"Perhaps we…should talk," he said.

He felt her shiver at his touch, and realized it might not have been the right move. Other than the knuckle sandwich he'd given her way back in high school, he had never touched her.

***

They walked casually along the sidewalk running the front of the supermarket-turned barracks. Considering the expansive parking lot before it a plethora of crude tents, tin sheds, piles of building material and squat makeshift silos of trash, the walkway they traversed was swept impeccably clean. Where thick sheet metal barricades didn't obscure, the painted exterior storefront walls were white. They had installed heavy duty plate-glass mirrored windows. Billet wondered how many people peered upon them as they went by. The Regan family portion of the building was the size and girth of a massive cathedral. Its mountainous shadow loomed over the southwestern half of the grounds like a bird of prey. Vulture-like, Billet thought.

"They are not Gurk soldiers, I can assure you of that," Rebecca said as they stopped before a set of large steel double doors, replying to Billet's question about the noticeable population of ZT's.

Jake knew otherwise but didn't want to press the matter. He'd seen the pistol LaFleur wielded, and the shambling troopers as they were paraded within view, as if taunting him. They wore Gurk combat uniforms. He supposed they could have come in torn and stripped of whatever uniform they'd worn before, and simply decked out with stolen military regalia. But the small force Regan showcased… Jake couldn't figure where they had gotten them if not from local supply.

Regardless of the zombie troopers in their midst, he also wondered what she subjected herself to in relation. He decided he really didn't want to pursue *that* subject either.

"Your father has a good thing here," Billet said. "I'd hate to see any trouble come to you if City Central ever got curious."

"I am thrilled you're showing your concern for me," Rebecca cooed, eyes flitting to his lips as she leaned in close.

Even her breath reeked of that tarry smell. Bile rose in his throat again as he tried to nonchalantly crane his neck away.

"Are you curious?" She said almost nose to nose.

If she was trying to get a rise out of him, he would have to dig *it* out from his abdomen with a pair of tongs once he'd left the place.

"Curious?" Billet responded, taking a step back. His reward was a jab in the back by one of Rebecca's gun-toting bullies.

"Curious enough to report back to your higher ups and bring the big city's military might down upon us?" Rebecca answered.

Billet relaxed and considered the statement.

"I'm just a grunt, ma'am." Billet said, reverting to a more general soldier's stance. "I know my place in the bigger scheme of things. And we're out here enough where I know, if suspected I might be bringing certain Intel back to the main camp…"

Though serious, Rebecca eyed him suspiciously.

"I'm sure my crew and I wouldn't be long for this world if we were known for just being out and about gathering information on things going on outside Grand Rapids," he finished.

Placing her hand on the door handle, she turned away from him. He looked at the doors, envisioning what would happen if he went inside with her. Though she never had him, he knew she always got what she wanted. He envisioned himself, wrapped in those sickly gray arms.

She spun on him, her talon of a fingernail nearly cutting

across the bridge of his nose.

"You lie!," she screamed, causing both Billet and the guards to flinch.

"I've been keeping tabs on you, Jacob Ethan Billet," she continued. "I would know if you'd come by here before, and I assure you, you would've been made to stop versus some 'accident' that brought you here now.

"Grand Rapids only has a few of the big personnel carriers like yours. I would know if you and your crew were about.

"If it were an actual distribution run you're on, you wouldn't be the only lone vehicle, and I see no escort vehicles," she finished.

She swept her hand out, drawing Billet's attention to the BRV-O, Blast Resistant Vehicle-Offroad, ground vehicles and a lone deuce-and-a-half in the parking lot. Reganshire had a small fleet of these vehicles including some old Humvees. And, yes, a typical D-run got you a couple smaller armed escorts...typically. Billet ventured out plenty of times on lone patrols with the Huron and his crew, though it was not the norm. News of such excursions usually weren't broadcast as more shiftless folk looked for opportunities to gain such a prize if it rolled alone.

"Well, it isn't much of a distribution run now since your people took half of my load," Billet said.

"I am saying I would have known if *you* were coming by, and I did not. I am saying you are *not* on a distribution run, because the GRCC wouldn't risk sending one of their last big transports through our territory by its lonesome." Her tone started to rise in pitch towards hysterics. Her guards shuffled nervously.

She pointed an accusing finger at him again, and screeched, "I *know* you are on a different mission, and not this oh-so-merciful excursion you claim."

Billet shook his head slowly. This is why, minus the Collindale incident, Aikens job would have been being able to have them roll through without hesitation.

"We've received Intel that the Regent of Muskegon is secretly being delivered home by means of GRCC transport," Rebecca continued, ice rolling from her verbal deliverance.

Jake's neck muscles tensed and froze.

"It's a shame his helicopter got shot down," she said, smirking dangerously. "But you wouldn't be the one so *nice*," She hissed out, "And taking the scourge of West Michigan home, would you?" She scratched a talon under his chin. "Hmmm? Sweetie?"

Billet opened his mouth to reply, fighting against a jaw locked by rising dread.

"Has the transport been searched thoroughly?" she howled, turning to her men.

The poor guards who hadn't been there when the Huron arrived shrugged with sorry looks, wishing they could answer her absolutely. They recoiled as if slapped when she crashed through them and bellowed, "Has anyone thoroughly checked the fucking transport?"

The throng hurried behind the woman bearing down on the HTV, forgetting Billet for the moment.

"Hostiles incoming. Hostiles incoming," Jake said, tapping his earbud. He followed after Rebecca. "Stokes, make sure the *cargo* is shored up."

Billet watched his gunner casually walk and then hurriedly disappear around the rear of the transport.

Phelps dropped from the engine compartment, flicking the heavy hatch door closed with her booted foot. With her sleeves rolled up, she wiped hands on a greasey rag, wringing it tightly as she watched the approaching throng. Her dark arms bulged with corded muscle.

LaFleur and Mulholland intercepted the enraged woman as both groups met a few steps away from the front corner of the transport.

"Commander, when you let this vehicle inside our gates, did

you check it thoroughly for contents *and* personnel?" Rebecca said craning her head back to look up into LaFleur's suddenly worried face.

With chest thrust out and arms at his side, LaFleur stood statue still. Only his mouth moved. "Yes, Miss Regan. Normal cargo, which we acquired much of, ma'am," he waited for an encouraging reaction from the woman, but it didn't come so he added quickly: "and all personnel accounted for: commander, driver, navigator. And gunners, ma'am." He shot a quick look to Mulholland at last comment.

Rebecca peered questionably at the massive vehicle.

"And no one else within, around, or under?" She inquired.

LaFleur jumped as if he'd just been kicked in the balls.

"Uh. No, ma'am." The big man answered, eyes darting until her gaze fell upon him and he again acquired the rigidity of a concrete pillar.

Billet squeezed his way through the shoulder-to-shoulder crowd, stopping within an arms length of Rebecca. Her eyes met his, and a devious smile spread her ashen countenance.

"I want your crew out, front and center, Captain." Rebecca hissed, all affection withdrawn, back to conventions.

Shit, Billet thought. He tapped his earbud, and said aloud, "All crew out for inspection. All… crew."

He looked across the compound to the gallows Rebecca had earlier spoke of. His neck started to itch.

Phelps pushed her way through, snarling at a few men who gazed upon her lustily.

Mulholland patted his towering friend's shoulder as he moved around him.

"There's a bounty on Lettner. Bring him in alive or dead," Rebecca said aloud though her gaze fell on Billet. "If he fell into our hands, I'd of course rather gut him alive and let my hounds dine on him a bit while he watches his intestines gnawed."

Jake saw Aikens standing amidst the gathering mob. The man gave him a partial salute and nod. He'd maintain his mole status, and send word of Billet's failure back to Grand Rapids.

Stokes appeared round the rear of the transport, followed by a hooded Lettner.

Billet noticed the regent's right hand at his belt, covering the concealed pistol he had been given from the cab's sidearm box. A big lot of nothing that would do for him.

Klaxons erupted across the compound, howling painfully in the mobs ears as a light post nearby held one of the siren bells. The milling crowd looked to one another as if they weren't sure what was going on.

"They're bringing the whole place down on us," Stokes said just loud enough to be heard over the din of the siren. He and Lettner stopped short of the back tread.

Billet planned on seeing his wife and son sometime in the afterlife, Lord willing. His expectation though was it wouldn't happen under circumstances like this, nor so soon.

CHAPTER SIX
The Last Campus Party

They had not parked far from one of the two Reganshire "north gates." Only a small building that used to be a jewelry store and a line of scrubby trees blocked Billet's view of the sudden hubbub at the northwestern-most gate.

Pushing through the crowd, panting, barely able to get the words out, a gate guard ran up to the towering LaFleur.

"Commander, the salvage crew from this morning…" A fresh howling siren cut the man off. A badly rusted EMS van rolled through the compound, parting the group again as it hurried to the north gate.

Billet could see two light tactical vehicles, a BRV-O and an old open-roofed HMMWV, or Humvee, on the other side of the gatehouse fence along with a flurry of activity. He began to think the blaring warning sirens were now not a herald to their doom as he watched more medical personnel rush towards the gate.

"Commander," the guardsman began again. "Only a quarter of the salvage team has returned with…" Still trying to catch his breath, the man grabbed his knees to regain control. Jake thought the guy might lose his lunch as his face lost color. "They say they were ambushed just outside the VSU communal…"

It was then the man realized one of the Regan family stood near. He snapped to attention, his chest still heaving.

"What is this you say?" Rebecca said, her attention fully on the guard and activity at the gate.

Jake took the moment to catch his own breath, trying to calm his nerves and heartbeat.

"Mistress Regan," the man partially bowed, "It seems the scientists of the VSU communal have unleashed another creature. I have not acquired the full report yet, but the university campus and Allendale is under siege."

"By what?" Rebecca said. Her tone one of building fury again.

She turned and started walking towards the gate where the EMS vehicle had stopped. The gathering flowed with her. With long strides and trying to catch a glimpse of what was ahead, LaFleur checked himself to not break pace and walk ahead of his leader.

Billet moved along with the group. As he passed Stokes at the rear of the transport, he tapped his earbud so the communication went only to his crew. "Get any gear stowed. Be ready for the worst."

Lettner peered from under the hood of the flak jacket. His furrowed brow showed he was none too happy.

At the moment, Billet could care less.

"A giant what?" Rebecca was heard saying incredulously as Billet caught up to her, LaFleur, and his stammering guards.

"Another mutation, but this one supposedly larger than a full grown elephant and twice as fast," the guard replied.

"A giant bull?" LaFleur said.

Roughly a dozen of the group, along with Rebecca, Billet and her guards, filtered through the enclosure and out onto the open street. A string of armed men stood along the perimeter. They kept their eyes on their surroundings lest shamblers appeared from the wreckage of the village outside the compound. Billet hadn't seen any Feral zombs en masse wandering around the exterior of the village. Like wild animals, they avoided populated areas unless exceptionally hungry. The areas between the vestiges of living, breathing humanity were the places one had to be especially leery when traveling. Still, being cautious usually meant well-armed and able to survive another day.

They moved around the two returned vehicles: a BRV-O and a Humvee.

The BRV-O, a replacement for the aged Humvee line of military Light Tactical Vehicles, still ran though it steamed and hissed from a broken radiator. The beefy vehicle appeared to have run a losing gauntlet through a gunnery range. It was a hard top model with a small roof-mounted gun turret. Billet had seen rollovers look prettier. The vehicle's top was crushed and damaged to the point it hung by a small seam of metal on one side. The crumpled turret stood void of weapon, its stanchion shorn off as if something had bitten it. The woodland camouflaged paint scheme was splattered with an addition of blood red.

The Humvee faired just a very small fraction better than its companion. It rode on three wheels; the passenger's side fourth down to the rim, smoking and giving off an acrid scent of burnt rubber. Creased and crumpled, the hood remained closed by single hold-down. There wasn't a quarter panel or section of body not severely dented. Along the passenger-side side panels until the tattered rear wheel, a long crease ran the length. Something big and sharp had dragged along it to create such a jagged line in the metal.

The men took the brunt of whatever had attacked them. The EMS crew pulled two bodies from the back of the BRV-O, covered, dead. Blood ran from beneath the silent black tarps. White as a bed sheet, a man was helped off the bigger vehicle, holding his right arm, a makeshift tourniquet at the elbow, his hand and forearm missing. The rest of the men and women taken from the vehicles, bloody and bruised, glanced about with blank stares; some with emotion choked and awestruck looks as if they were in disbelief of still being amongst the living.

Billet had witnessed normal-sized animal mutations from the old zoo, brutal zombie attacks inside and outside the city, and violent scrimmages between men. It was the typical scenario of a world in complete chaos. This incoming Reganshire group had seen something else entirely. They had been pulled through the intake of the bus from Hell, twisted, torn, burned, bloodied and shit out the exhaust pipe.

"…Heard it, but the gawddamn thing came out of nowhere," a man said coming from the Humvee, his arms looped over two assisting Reganite. His left leg dangled at an odd angle just below the knee.

"Smoke and small explosions were coming from the VSU campus," a woman said also being helped from the same vehicle. She wore a large bloody gash on the side of her head; the sweat and blood matting her hair made it look like she'd just stepped from a shower. "The convoy turned down 48th Avenue when…"

"A herd of cows attacked you," Rebecca said sarcastically. She folded her arms across her chest, proud of herself, and looked to see who laughed at her remark.

The woman sneered, raised an index finger indicating the correct number, and while the other woman still gloated, lowered the index and momentarily flipped up the middle.

"A bull. A big ass bull." The woman said as one of the EMT's saw to her head wound. "Once we saw the size of the thing, Butkus turned us around. Started shooting. It didn't slow the thing in the least."

"Butkus," LaFleur chimed in, stepping closer and peering from vehicle to vehicle as if missing something. "What happened to him?"

The woman glanced over her shoulder from where the convoy had come. She hesitated a moment, trembling a little before snapping herself back to the present.

"The thing took out almost every vehicle. Butkus stayed back with the few who weren't as badly wounded, to guard them from any of the lunatics from the VSU compound…if there is anyone. Place pretty much is smoking rubble," she said, grimacing as a gauze bandage was applied to her head. "We spotted some Ferals on the way in, so I am sure he's keeping watch for them too until a rescue party can be sent."

Billet watched as the last Reganite grunt was hauled off the back of the BRV-O. He was alive, but an assisting man held a lump of bloody bandages over the other's midsection, appearing to be keeping the poor devil's guts from falling out. He had been gored by something the circumference of a thick fence post. A pair of medics helped get the man on a gurney as they passed Billet.

"Don't want to be no zombie or no bloodhound, Sam. Put a bullet in my head before that, okay?" The mortally wounded fellow sobbed to the other who helped hold in his innards.

Jake glanced at Rebecca standing a few feet away. She looked down at the blood on the roadway, staring as if in a trance. She licked her pale red lips, scratching at the weeping bandage on her own diseased arm. The realization came to him, though it been a niggling thought just a while back. Now, he knew it to be true. The fresh anger stirring inside him made his hand slip to his sidearm. He should have put a bullet in the bitch's head right then and there for what she had done, and was doing.

Everyone in the military was vaccinated back when the viral biological blight and the war on the undead had been at its worse. Unless a soldier experienced a fatal head wound or was blown to bits, the discovered side effects of the injected vaccine was a state of semi-undeath. The governing heads found this to be an answer to the problem when dwindling enlistment occurred. It didn't make you immortal, but kept you living with all skills intact and a tidal wave of emotions as the memories of your former life drown, and the hunger and aggression flooded in. However, its knowledge killed further recruiting, and moral trust in the establishment, and left bitterness with the already enlisted. The military discontinued further use of the vaccine, though it was still used to further treat the undead soldiers, the ZT's, thus still on the market.

But what the woman was doing...

Like all good drugs, the serum slipped out into the black market arena. Illegal to have, some folks wanted semi-immortality no matter what the cost. Abuse slowly broke down healthy living tissue. Abusers were usually caught just by their appearance. Being caught sentenced one to execution by a bullet to the brain.

But if one was influential enough and had a father in a high seat of authority...

Billet moved his hand away from his pistol. Rebecca Regan would get hers, or someone would get her. But after stealing another glance at the destroyed convoy, he decided he had other more pressing concerns to deal with.

"We need to get back there and retrieve Butkus and the others," LaFleur said to Rebecca.

She snapped out of her trance, eyes darting to see if anyone was looking at her. Her ashen cheeks darkened in a faint blush as she bitingly replied: "They are probably dead already, and we don't have further vehicles to waste or jeopardize."

LaFleur huffed, waving a hand towards the compound. "We have another fleet in storage."

The big man tried to do the right thing. Billet felt a new sense of respect for the towering gorilla.

Rebecca stalled, and then said, switching from bitch to innocence: "I'll have to wait and ask daddy."

LaFleur drooped. "You know your father won't send a patrol party out at night..."

Angry rumblings coursed through the crowd. Rebecca lost her smug look, surprising Jake with an expression of sudden worry. Power and control was important to the woman, but it appeared she might have enough actual humanity left to understand full abuse of that power could hurt her. Billet grinned with the thought: what would dear father say if he found *her* swinging from the gallows?

She took LaFleur aside. Billet could not hear their conversation over the rest of the crowd.

None of this bode well. He, his crew, and Lettner were heading right by VSU and through Allendale. Looking at his watch, they were already running behind. He did not plan on deeply venturing out in "the wilds" once it got dark either, and the afternoon hours were slipping away fast. So far, it'd been a shit of a mission.

And the worst part yet to be carried out, Jake thought, as he looked back at the Huron.

He noticed Rebecca turning away from her giant gate commander, turning her gaze on Billet. A huge shit-eating grin curled her pale, cracked lips, and LaFleur looked at him as if silently voicing his apologies.

"Captain Billet…" Rebecca said.

"Sonuvabitch," Jake grumbled behind clenched teeth, knowing what was to come.

"I need to commandeer your vehicle," she finished.

"Gawddamnsonuvabitch."

***

"Vesper sending the message?" Loutonia asked as she stared out the driver's viewport at the road ahead.

The Reganshire compound shrank behind them, however LaFleur and a dozen soldiers sat atop and within the transport. A single BRV-O—one in good repair that Rebecca felt nice enough to let LaFleur "borrow"—followed behind them with four more men. All were well-armed with a mechanic and two medics in the group to see to the busted and broken once they hooked up with Stefan Butkus and his salvage crew.

Billet looked at Lettner who sat in the cab's navigator seat, stewing with arms folded across his chest. The regent sneered at him when he noticed eyes upon him.

Jake ignored him, turning his attention to one of the side viewports and peering out. Only woodland and a few dilapidated estates were along this stretch of M-45. They rolled on almost to the peak of a steep hill before going down into the Grand River Valley again. The remnants of an old greenhouse stood at the peak of the hill.

"Yeah. I'm sure the recipient won't be too thrilled," Jake replied to Phelps. "Running a little behind as we are."

"I've never seen such barbarism," Lettner spoke up.

"What?" Billet said, surprised by the man's statement. "This is what we've come to, an 'eye for an eye,' and all that. Communities looking after each other, greedily holding on to whatever they can get their hands on."

Lettner looked at him with suspicion in his eyes. If he suspected a slam, that's exactly what it was.

"Who is this 'Vesper' you are talking about?" The regent asked.

Phelps looked back at him. It didn't really matter if Lettner knew, he wouldn't be able to use the Intel where he was going.

"It's our contact in Reganshire. If the episode with the engine hadn't happened, he would've made sure we passed through Regan's place without having to stop. Which would have been fine with me," Billet said, the vision of Rebecca Regan's corpse-flesh image in his mind's eye, making him shiver.

"He's our messenger until we reach the lakeshore, making sure your pick-up knows our whereabouts and when we'll be there," Billet finished.

Lettner seemed satisfied with that.

A knock came at the closed cab door. Before Billet could grab the handle, the door opened. Mulholland stooped and leaned his head in.

"LaFleur wants to talk to you, Captain," the gunner said.

"I'll be right up."

Mulholland backed out of the entry. Jake could see the half dozen Reganshire troopers peering back at him.

"Stay put, please." He said to Lettner, knowing the belligerent and pompous man itched to walk right into the lion's den. And the lion had guns.

The regent grumbled something and looked away.

"Keep sharp," he said to Loutonia. "Oh, and I see you got your tool box back." The tool kit the patch-eyed Reganite had claimed sat stowed again in the driver's compartment.

"Yeah, the grabby bugger was nice enough to give them back… with interest," she said, digging into her pants pocket, coming out with a fist. She opened her hand to reveal several blood-stained gold-capped teeth.

"Barbaric," Lettner snorted before returning to his cross-armed stewing.

***

Lucius LaFleur sat on the back of the transport, one leg hanging over the deck and the other with foot resting on the lid. An assault rifle rested between thigh and belly. Mulholland stood in the rear gunner's hatch. Their conversation ceased when Billet rose from the opposite rearward hatch.

Jake surveyed the handful of men on the Huron's roof. Each held their weapons—rifles and small automatic weapons—tight. Each also tightly gripped the rungs lining the perimeter of the transport's central roof cargo doors. Clustered with clumps of weeds and broken roadbed, at 30 miles per hour, the ride top-side was slightly precarious.

"What can I do you for?" Billet said to the big Reganite.

LaFleur nodded over his shoulder. "VSU is still smoking badly."

Billet looked to the west, in the direction they were heading.

Roughly a mile away, black smoke boiled from several places on the opposite hill side. The thick ebon streamers rose up to darken the already hazy sky. The dense tree line along the ridge obscured any sign of the burning buildings.

"Appears the goodly scientists got their asses handed to them by their own creation finally," Jake answered, more sarcastic than he meant to sound.

LaFleur looked sheepishly at Mulholland, and returned his gaze to the road beneath them.

"But I don't think that is why you called me back here," Billet said. He cast his lanky gunner a cross look, who returned it with a shrug of shoulders and innocent shake of his head. A growl of irritation rose in Jake's throat.

"I know what your additional *cargo* is," LaFleur said still with his eyes to the road.

Jake cast a frosty gaze at Mulholland again. Mulholland shook his head obstinately like Saint Peter in the garden. The gunner wasn't the one who spilled the beans.

"And how did you come across this information?" Billet asked.

"I saw his face when he stepped out of the vehicle for a brief second, when Miss Regan called you all out."

So much for stealth and secrecy, Billet thought.

"Who else knows about this?" He glanced at the other Reganites who seemed to take no notice of their conversation.

"Probably nobody. Nobody in this group anyway," Lucius replied. "Not too many people know what the man looks like."

Billet remained silent.

"We received information he'd be on ground transport back to Muskegon," LaFleur said as the transport thumped over a chunk of roadbed, nearly dislodging him from his perch. He pulled himself back so he sat with a larger part of his body atop the roof. He continued: "All the gate commanders were shown pictures of him in the off chance he came through our area. Mr. Regan sent out a hundred men to the I-96 corridor to cut him off, bring him in and dole out his own justice since Mayor Honeywell and Grand Rapids wouldn't."

Mulholland's stood in wide eyed shock.

Billet again cast a wary eye at the men on his rooftop, and then back to LaFleur who didn't move a muscle.

"Is there going to be trouble, Mr. LaFleur?" Jake started to raise his pistol to clear the hatch line.

Billet looked at Mulholland the same time Lucius glanced his friend's way. Mulholland's hands casually held his machine gun grips. Both men shared a pained expression, realizing their friendship may not have been as solid as they thought. Jake couldn't see his gunner opening up point-blank unless his opposition was ready to do the same. LaFleur wore a mask of dejection.

"Ed told me he'd follow you to Hell and back," Lucius said, eyes to the road again.

The road sloped gently downward towards the river valley. In the distance, before the next hill climb that would bring the Huron and its escort alongside the VSU property, a four-lane bridge spanned the river.

LaFleur continued: "I understand how you are a respectable man, but I don't see how, in good conscience, you can transport a mass murderer like William Lettner without issue. And knowing, at some point, he might try to do the same deed on inland towns, even Grand Rapids, and people…"

"Oh, I have no doubt he'd love to scrub the whole of West Michigan free of the remaining zombie populace, and any other obstacles he feels he shouldn't have to endure," Billet said watching the top of the hill shrink away. For a moment he felt as if he were actually sinking.

He re-holstered his sidearm and brought his hands up to grip the rim of the hatch.

"And the reason why I took the task of returning him home

has nothing to do with respect or good conscience." Jake said, trying to keep emotions out of it. It didn't matter if LaFleur knew what was going down.

"You let this out of the bag, and I'll bury you personally," Billet said with assured promise.

LaFleur looked threatened and tense, until, in a low voice, Jake added, "The regent won't be going home."

Both Mulholland and Lucius peered at him aghast.

"Going home, but not the way he expects, and not back to any position of power," Jake said. He had to look away from the gaze of his own man, and pick his words carefully. "We were assigned the task of taking Lettner home. Luckily we did avoid the I-96 corridor as that was the course set by my superiors. Our new rendezvous point, to Lettner's knowledge, is to drop him off south of Grand Haven, and his people will take him from there.

Jake turned back to Mulholland, though his words were for both men. "He's actually going to be picked up before we officially enter NSC land, by his own council members. He has a few high profile surviving opponents in the NSC who've been waiting for an opportunity to unseat him without him getting a leg up and taking them out.

"I was contacted right after I signed us up for the mission," Billet said straight at Mulholland. "We'll be getting a little extra than standard pay when the cargo is delivered."

The young gunner looked like he'd been slapped.

"I apologize for not informing you of all the details," Jake said to Mulholland.

"We'll not be able to go back to Grand Rapids," Mulholland said.

The young soldier didn't have ties in town anyway, Billet thought. If any of his crew had real ties in the city, he would have found a reason to not have included them on the mission. They were all in the same boat, family and friends either far away, or dead and gone.

"We'll be all right," Jake said, exuding assurance on the outside for his crew member's sake. Behind the mask, and not a fortune teller, he felt little of that guarantee.

"Stokes and Phelps know?" Eddie asked.

Billet felt a small sense of relief as the gunner didn't appear too upset in being slightly deceived.

"Phelps knew up front as it's her rig," Billet answered him. "Stokes, no. But I think he wouldn't care anyway with his penchant for wanting to shoot things."

Mulholland didn't appear to find his commander's attempt at humor amusing.

"We're going to be picked up by NSC allies?" Mulholland asked.

"Basically. Yes."

"Beachfront homes and Pronto Pups," Mulholland said cracking a half-smile. "I could live with that."

"What's going to happen to us?" LaFleur broke in. "Seems I'm suddenly between a rock and a hard place."

Billet rubbed at his chin. Back when they arrived at the Reganshire village, he would have thought of a way to sweep the big man and his men from the transport and leave them behind in whatever shape he left them. However, in retrospect, LaFleur and his men were another bunch of poor grunts like him, doing what they had to do to survive and sometimes making the hard choices that didn't necessarily make life easy.

"We'll see what's left of your other guy's squad, and decide from there," Billet said. "If worse comes to worse, we'll cart ya back as close to your village as we can. I'll tell you what though, if you dump me into the hands of Silas's daughter..."

The big man exchanged an unspoken nod of understanding and allegiance, and appeared to shiver himself with the thought. "Yeah, there *are* some things worse than the old man."

***

They made the bottom of the hill. To the south, an old housing development encircled a man-made lake. The once elegant and expensive homes had succumbed to vacancy and time. On the opposite side of M-45, if homes had existed there, they had long since been retaken by nature. Even the paved roadway heading north lay broken and almost completely overgrown in a tangle of trees and tall grass.

"Captain, slight situation here," Phelps said under a pop of static in Billet's earbud.

"What is it?" His reply interrupted as the HTV gently jumped, bucking him slightly against the hatch coaming.

"Oh shit!" One of LaFleur's roof-mounted men exclaimed, quickly drawing up his legs from hanging over the side of the transport.

Billet didn't have to see what troubled the man, along with the others who were also squirming away from the roof's edge, as he, LaFleur and Mulholland discovered what they had ran over.

Like a mashed possum, but human-sized and gray of skin, a zomb lay in a twisted pan-caked mess as they rolled on.

Jake climbed out of the rear hatch, crouched and teetered his way towards the front of the vehicle. He flinched when Stokes, manning his usual front gun turret, squeezed off several rounds towards the roadway ahead.

"Gawddamnit, knock that shit off. You wanna bring them all in?" Jake snapped at the gunner.

A roof-seated Reganite screamed as a bony hand pulled him from the rooftop. Trying to leap to his companion's rescue, the man next to him went over the side with him.

LaFleur bellowed with rage, getting up on a bended knee and hefting his assault rifle.

"Ferals." Jake said under his breath as the living men pulled to the road were torn to pieces by the zombie pack suddenly swarming them from ditch and tree-line.

Stokes looked at him, giving him pleading puppy dog eyes.

Kidding or not with the ridiculous look, Billet gave a single nod to the trigger-happy gunner. "Go ahead. Let 'em have it," he ordered. "No auto-cannon. You might hit the LTV."

The sergeant deflated a bit, but went to work.

Phelps didn't slow as they fired and fought through the throng of rotters.

"Where're they all coming from?" A Reganite marksman said, coming to the roof as LaFleur called out to target the zombies attacking the LTV behind them.

A face of sagging flesh popped up on the edge of the roof between Stokes and Billet. Stokes didn't notice, sweeping his quad MG's in front of the transport.

Billet leaned forward and pressed the business end of his pistol against the snarling zomb's forehead. He pulled the trigger. The creature fell backwards, dropping towards the pavement, a gory streamer of rotted brain matter trailing behind it.

Jake glanced at the black smoke clouds huffing from the VSU compound. The place looming ever closer, up the next hill.

"Even the dead don't want to deal with whatever's up there," Billet replied as he shot another decaying climber from the side of the Huron. If the things wanted a ride out, they were asking to go the wrong way.

Another man went over the side screaming and firing blindly as another Feral leapt and pulled him off.

Stokes roared as a rotter sprang up, latching onto his hatch coaming. Not able to fire at that angle, he let go of the gun and jammed his gloved hand into the zomb's face. He drove his middle and ring finger into the thing's eye sockets, thumb angled down over the creature's chin, gripping its face as if holding a bowling ball.

"Try and get the grab on me will ya, motherfucker," he snarled as he drew his serrated recon Bowie knife from his belt sheath. With

ferocity matching his undead adversary, he sawed into its neck. He ignored the spray of gore as the head flopped over like an unhinged soup can lid.

Punching the zombie off and away from him, the Huron did the rest as the zomb fell into the churning tracks and was ground to red paste.

"Their swarming the BRV," LaFleur shouted between the singular punching barks of Mulholland's guns.

The gunner stayed dead-on target, firing short precision-placed bursts, hitting every time and keeping the individual shamblers off the LTV behind them. Solid and stout, the Z's would need a can opener to actually get inside it, if they got past the men firing point-blank in their face. Still, the BRV-O held LaFleur's only medics for the trip.

Shell casings bounced off the rooftop of the transport. Billet watched them spin and bounce. If the men kept expending ammo like they were—looking to all sides of the carrier, and what was still coming across the bridge and fields—Jake feared it might be a prolonged and costly fight along all avenues.

"Phelps, tell your navigator to get off his ass, and then drop the back gate to about crate width," Billet said into the comm.

"We're unloading the main package early?" Phelps returned.

Billet went backwards as a Feral came up over the side, taking him down to the steel rooftop. His head slammed to the hard metal surface. A big star flash bloomed before his eyes as his brain rattled in his skull. Raking at him, Jake grappled with the creature to keep its claw-like digits from his throat. He couldn't get his gun in line to shoot and swore loudly as the thing swiped across his head, deeply gashing his forehead from temple to temple. Warm blood ran down from his wound into his eyes. Blinded, he grabbed the zomb by its neck and to smash the butt of his pistol against its head. Sharp, broken teeth snapped at his face.

Jake opened one eye, blinking away the blood. Above him,

to the north, a jagged hole opened in the clouds. A stab of sunlight broke through, beaming down to some unknown location far away. His grandmother used to say, whenever sunbeams shone down to earth, Heaven searched for new angels to bring into their cast.

Probably why the beam of light didn't shine down on him.

His thoughts drifted to his wife and son.

Getting closer now.

Roughly 15 miles away, beyond the VSU and Allendale compounds, they were there, waiting for him. His angels.

So tired.

Lettner had to die.

"Captain!"

LaFleur's booming voice shook Billet from his fever dream. Already the wound from the zomb infected him, and his body valiantly fought against it.

Propped on his knees, Lucius tore the seething FZ from Jake. The big man twisted and launched it over the side.

"Unload all but a half dozen crates," Billet said in a weak growl into his throat mic. He could barely stand. His hand trembled as he holstered his gun and wiped at his forehead. His fingers came back sticky and red. He wanted to slide down into the bowels of the Huron and sleep in its belly forever.

"The Captain and Stokes are scratched and got the bug," Billet heard Mulholland say in his earbud. Though the gunner's position was nearly beside him, still firing into the zombies, the Lance Corporal's voice sounded far away.

The big transport lurched forward even as the heavy rear door screeched partially open.

"Fuck this," Jake heard his driver respond as crates rolled and bounced from behind the vehicle.

The Huron sped up.

Billet watched the LTV swerve left and right to avoid the sudden avalanche of meat crates. He heard a scream and saw another of LaFleur's men on the roadside, immediately lost under a tide of Ferals. Stoke's quad MG's barked long and rapidly. Chunky geysers of wood and meat erupted all over the road behind them, and like hungry cattle to a feed trough, Jake watched as a mass of galloping FZ's hurried to the red mess.

Jake wiped more blood from his eyes as the transport seemed to move unnaturally fast, faster than it should be able to go. His hand felt leaden, strength drained. The Huron tilted sideways underneath him.

"I got you, Captain," Mulholland said as Jake tilted back into his arms.

Billet saw Stokes, bloody as he, sinking down into the hatchway. A Reganite soldier guided him down. "Don't touch me, man. This is a trip," Stokes said, his eyes rolling up into the back of his head.

LaFleur and Mulholland lowered Billet over of the rear of the transport. His mind reeled, panicking, but he could do nothing if they decided to throw him off, abandon him. He looked up numbly at Mulholland. Did the man hate him for not telling him the full truth of their mission?

"You got meds to bring him back?" LaFleur said close to Billet's face. The big man's voice ebbed in and out. "We'd be shot if wounded like that."

Mulholland smiled down at Jake, his teeth like fangs. His lips moved, but Billet could not hear the words as the roar of the twin diesels drowned out his senses. He felt hands grasp his legs, pulling him down.

Glancing up as he sank down, Jake saw the sunbeam blink out and the sky grow dark. Then oblivion swallowed him into its ebon maw.

***

Billet woke to the dim light of the transport's interior and the rear hatch fully open. Someone held his face over a bucket. Senses returning, his head pound and heart jackhammered uncomfortably in his chest, but it could have been worse. Angled so he wouldn't choke on his own vomit, the hands holding him let him up. He turned over and sat on his rump, suddenly aware of a crowd around him. He touched his forehead, feeling the plump, tender line of stitched flesh where the zombie had raked him.

Another wave of nausea surged from his constricting stomach. He quickly brought his left hand to the meaty part of his shoulder and peeled off the med-pack.

"Enough of that," he said, rising up on unsteady feet. He latched onto the bulkhead until he got his bearings. The vaccine coursing through his system, letting him take blow after blow from the land and those infected didn't play well with other intervening medicines. The medi-packs hammered home the adrenaline and other healing chems needed to get a soldier back on their feet, but it left a hell of a sour gut and rancid taste on the tongue. Standing nearby, LaFleur offered a supportive arm as Jake moved to his locker, dug out a crumpled tube of toothpaste and squeezed a dollop into his mouth.

"Where we at?" Jake asked LaFleur then ran his finger about his teeth and tongue. He swallowed, grimacing with the action but his mouth didn't taste like ass anymore.

The door to the head flew open and Stokes stepped out, face pasty, but slowly returning to color. His face glistened with sweat and the first aid salve he had been slathered with. His right shirtsleeve was missing to his shoulder blade, the dirty tee underneath caked in dried blood. He looked as if he had chased a fart through a keg of nails, and lost, his right arm showcasing his only serious wound. A weaved black stitch ran from shoulder to elbow, holding a line of red puckered flesh together.

"That blew...literally," Stokes said, pushing his way through the Reganites who looked at him with slack jaws.

The squat gunner gave Billet and LaFleur a nod and climbed

back up into his gun station.

Billet glanced up at Lucius, the big man's brow furrowed as his gaze focused at the front of the Huron. Jake turned to see Lettner, hood pulled back, glaring back at the man.

Though a pair of Reganshire men stood next to the regent, they didn't seem to take notice of who he was.

"Where we at?" Jake said again. He shared glances with Lettner and Lucius, waiting for an answer.

"At the top of the hill, not far from the VSU gate house," Lucius answered, finally tearing his eyes from the other man.

"What a mess," Stokes voice echoed through the hatchway.

Billet walked to the rear of the vehicle and stepped down onto the roadway. The LTV was parked behind them, the medics tending to a few men who had met worse fates than his own. Jake could hear the men groaning, still in their fever pitch to shake the infection. Non-military and not having the cursed vaccine in their system, the medi-packs would take a bit longer to work on them.

Mulholland met him as he stepped out from around the carrier. LaFleur moved next to his friend, watching the black plumes that rose from the VSU campus. The sound of flames crackling and popping rolled over the tree line and to their ears.

"Status?" Jake asked both men though his gaze fell on his rear gunner.

Mulholland cleared his throat. "Phelps is scraping the *bug* guts off the front of the rig. No opposition so far."

"I lost five of my men. Got three wounded who aren't going to be much help. Our vehicle is okay other than a few dents and dings," LaFleur added.

Jake looked over at the big BRV-O. The grill and fender had a few splatterings of red meat about them, from a zomb encounter or the exploding bins of Z-rations he wasn't sure.

"Better have your guys clean that gunk off before we go further or you'll be bait on a hook," Billet said.

He turned his full attention on Lucius. "How far did your men say they got before they were attacked?"

"They were beyond the gate," LaFleur answered, wringing his big hands nervously. "Then they got hit as they passed the old golf course."

Billet nodded and continued his walk around the Huron. He stopped in his tracks as he made his way to the front. Phelps came into view wearing a pair of bloodied welding gloves, her expression foul as if someone had pissed in her Cheerios.

"Captain," she nodded in salutation though grim of face.

Billet looked passed her, jaw hanging loose. "Holy shit."

The VSU east gate command post and guard barracks used to be an old frat house, and before that a historical home of some long residing Allendale family; both names and people long since forgotten. A white two-story home with a gabled roof, it had been maintained in pristine shape even when utilized by the current Valley State University residents.

The home now looked like it had been gently kissed by a wrecking ball. Repeatedly.

Billet chewed his lip as he gazed at the structure. The entire front face sagged into a pile of debris, like a tornado had sheared off the front, leaving the rest standing. The actual gate, which had been installed years ago, spanning the full length of the roadway, lay crumpled and twisted.

The commune of scientists were well known for driving heavily modified and armored older vehicles, Crown Vic's and Lincoln Continentals. A dozen of these vehicles were strewn about and discarded like child's toys. They rested on their sides, some burnt, some simply crushed flat. The vehicle's occupants had fared no better. Bodies lay everywhere: bent, broken and some even appeared trampled, mashed flat.

Billet felt half inclined to ask Phelps if she'd rolled their transport through here before he'd come out of his funk.

"Those crazy gene-splicers went beyond experimenting on wild Z's and animals…" Jake said, not sure what to say beyond that.

Though nothing moved in their immediate vicinity getting back behind some armor plating seemed a good idea.

"Let's load up and get moving. I still have a schedule to adhere to."

He could feel Mulholland and LaFleur's heated stare at his back, but ignored it. Damned either way he sliced it.

***

Sitting in the front commander's cupola, Jake slowly scanned the area as they rolled over and onward through the VSU east gate. Unlike the Collindale Outpost, that in his mind wasn't necessarily needed, he felt he committed a slight transgression with passing through the property gate without "signing in" (and most likely getting grilled) same as Reganshire. As they drove over the crumpled gate, passing the ruined command post, he expected armed men to run out, waving fist and weapon, calling for them to halt at once.

No one appeared.

Stokes manned his quads, eyes darting, sweating more bullets than his ammo box. Jake let a splinter of concern pass through him. Other than the sweats—from nerves or still fighting the wounds—the gunner appeared his normal hair-trigger self.

"Everyone stay frosty," Billet said into his throat mike.

LaFleur joined the men in the LTV. Jake turned, signaled to the Reganite soldiers remaining atop his rig, and made sure the big man and his group got the message to keep sharp.

Phelps weaved the Huron around the carnage. Whatever VSU let loose, it appeared everyone and everything had tried to escape it. Vehicles littered the roadway as well as bodies of the dead and the undead. Pulped and torn as they were, none of the bodies would be bothering anyone anymore. Crows and turkey buzzards warily circled the rolling clouds of ebon smoke rising from the campus proper, waiting.

"Commander," one of the Reganites perched behind Billet called to him. It was odd to hear someone other than his crew report to him as such. "That truck right there."

The man pointed at an old Chevy S-10 pickup resting on its side. Its undercarriage revealed a long scar of torn metal where something sharp and heavy had dragged across it.

The door emblem was what the Reganite pointed at. A black and white stencil of Engine House No. 5, the symbol of the Allendale-Robinson communal, showed plainly on the crumpled driver's side door.

"Either stolen or they came to assist their neighbors," Billet replied. He scanned the nearby bodies, searching for any sign of folks that might be wearing the same insignia. So utterly smashed and bloody, he couldn't make heads or tails of the mangled humanity. And he wasn't going to stop just yet and be more inquisitive.

Thunder sounded south of them, within the campus grounds. A bawling howl rose until it filled the air around them, and then echoed away into the distance.

"Jeezuz, what's that?" Phelps called from the cockpit.

The big transport wasn't going fast, careful as Phelps was to not roll across too many bodies. Everyone listened closely above the low gargle of the diesels. Another series of rumblings and what sounded like a building crashing down came to ear. Something within the compound still rampaged.

"Sounded like a big ass cow," Stokes said. His knuckles were white, holding the hand grips on the his guns. He lessened his death grip when he saw Billet looking at him.

"Lot of livestock around here," the Reganite beside Billet said. "Well, used to be anyway. We all try to maintain some animals within our own walls. VSU no different, except ya know they experimented on them too." The man's face wrinkled in disgust as he emitted that last sentence.

Crossing his hands over his chest with balled fists, Jake made sure Mulholland saw the gesture to "strap down," and watched as the gunner sent the same signal to LaFleur and the others in the LTV.

"Get yourself strapped in," Billet said lowering himself down into the guts of the Huron. "Not sure what we're going to run into, or to hightail away from."

The remaining Reganshire men were already nested in fold-down seat pans. They immediately started buckling themselves in.

Lettner sat in the seat he'd acquired since they'd left, but sat unharnessed and leaning forward with elbows on knees.

"Hey," Billet barked at the regent a little more aggressively than he intended. "That means you."

Lettner peered up at Jake with a double barrel middle-finger look in eyes and face.

Billet's anger flared. He clenched his teeth to keep from spewing a rash of obscenities at the pig-headed son of a bitch. Suddenly LaFleur's earlier words were rolling through his head: *transporting a mass murderer.* The Reganshire gate commander didn't know the half of Jake's reason, though it would surely come through the wire on the morn…if they even made it to mission's end.

He realized the reason for being so currently smoked. Nothing had gone as planned throughout the entire excursion, and whatever brought down the VSU campus and was tearing up Allendale assistance…

They'd stepped in the poop once they'd left the Grand Rapids city gate, and been swirling around like refuse in a wastewater stirring pot ever since.

And what lay at the far end of the mission's road?

Jake suddenly felt extremely tired, road weary, nerves stretched thin. It could be the recent wound still teasing at him. Fifteen miles was all there was between here and the drop off point. It wouldn't be long now. He told everyone travelling this route wouldn't bother him in the least. He had even told himself that.

It was a lie.

Perhaps it hadn't been a good idea to chart a course bringing him through his old homestead, through Lettner's "cleansed lands" with the man himself who had caused him and the area such heart-rending grief. But it was the reason Billet was bringing the regent "home." To end this, and bring closure to his own pain.

It was a flame and gasoline combo, and, feeling the burden grow heavier as the thought of the end drew near, Billet wasn't sure how long he could keep from blowing up on the guy.

"Strap in," Billet reiterated, eyes off the regent in fear he'd lose control and come down off his stand.

"Commander, I have visual on some Reganshire vehicles ahead," Phelps said through the comm.

Let him rattle around like a ball bearing in a dryer, Billet thought as he raised himself back topside.

LaFleur's driver must have seen their vehicles at the same time Phelps noticed them. The LTV charged forward, roaring around the Huron.

"So much for not attracting attention," Billet growled. "Pick it up a little, Phelps."

The transport immediately picked up speed to follow after the BRV-O. The men atop the carrier tensely held their weapons, ready for anything, hoping *anything* didn't come rushing out to meet them

***

Vehicles lay on their sides and on their rooftops. Hoods, side panels and undercarriages appeared torn, dented and crumpled. A scene similar to the rest of the roadway path, it changed as a few living subjects crawled from the roadside wreckage. They waved down the approaching vehicle.

"Get up close, and secure the perimeter," Billet ordered as

they rolled up to intercept LaFleur's halted group and emerging Reganshire survivors.

Another unholy bawl went up, making everyone go rigid. Stopped as they were near the corner of M-45 and 48th Avenue, everyone peered south in the direction in which the inhuman bellow rose.

"That just ain't natural," Stokes said, keeping his sight and his guns pointed southward.

Billet climbed down from the transport, pistol drawn, and headed over to where LaFleur and his medics were.

A small, older model Humvee lay on its rooftop in the drainage ditch. The side of the road dipped into a steep culvert, the vee it made from bank to bank had let the vehicle lay upside down and created a hidden shelter beneath. Luckily the season had been very dry. Only tall weeds and grass grew from the ditch.

"Butkus is alive and okay, other than a busted ankle," Lucius exclaimed as Jake carefully stepped down into the ditch. A body of another Reganshire man, arms missing and a bullet hole in the forehead, had not been so fortunate; a gray-skinned feral lay nearby with a caved-in face.

With LaFleur stepping in to assist, his medics dragged the other Reganshire commander from under the overturned Humvee. Butkus wasn't quite Lucius's size but still bigger and broader than Billet. Jake thought perhaps old man Regan, a fairly big man from what he recalled, picked his lieutenant's bigger than the usual lot of men. It surely garnered respect in Jake's book. Butkus sported a shaved head which revealed a number of bloody gashes and raised bruises.

"We need to get the hell outta here," Butkus said with a raspy voice as they gingerly dragged him up to road level. One of the medics handed him a canteen of water.

With assistance by some men who jumped down from the transport, two other men pulled themselves from beneath the wreckage. They looked pale and gaunt, sporting multiple cuts and contusions. They peered with wide eyes towards the smoking campus, almost too entranced and fear-filled to look in any other direction.

"What caused this mess?" LaFleur asked Butkus. "We haven't stopped weaving around bodies and wreckage since we entered the area."

They propped Butkus against the side of Huron. He swore and looked ready to punch one of the medics as they removed his boot and started work on his broken appendage. One gave him half a shot of morphine, which calmed him but left him lucid enough to tell his tale.

"We got through the gate without issue, though they searched us good," Butkus said as something cracked loudly in the distance, causing everyone to pause to look again towards the campus. The Reganite continued, not fazed: "Thought we were carrying that asshole from Muskegon. Supposedly they got word he might be in a convoy coming this way."

LaFleur shot a glance at Billet.

Billet returned a blank look. Inwardly, it didn't surprise him. Moles were everywhere. Everyone had one. Word could have come from anyone. Even his own plant in Reganshire, though he doubted it. He'd known Aikens too long. And, sure, anyone could be bought nowadays. Even so, if it had been his guy, they would have been smoked out long ago.

Plus convoy meant more than one vehicle. Whichever way the regent was to get home, everyone would be looking for a fully armed entourage, not one lone beast of a transport and her crew to defend the man. That would be assured suicide. The absurdity had crossed Jake's mind, but the cargo and the payout had been too alluring.

"Still, I got a funny feeling from the VSU guards when we passed through. You could tell they were all nervous about something, and we heard gun shots and what sounded like small explosions within their compound," Butkus said, lifting his hand and looking at it as if he wasn't sure it was his.

"We'd barely gotten halfway down the road when a whole lot of shit hit the fan. Suddenly there were rotters racing out all over the place, Ferals and a bunch of other abominations. It was easy pickings because they seemed more intent on getting out of there than chewin' on us.

"But then stuff really started blowing up, people running all over the place. Saw a lot of Allendale militia coming out of there, and not sure who fired the first shot at the other, but next thing they—VSU folk and us--are throwing lead at each other and the abominations coming out of the compound."

There had always been an uneasy truce between the VSU and Allendale communities. VSU with their modern research facilities, and Allendale who'd gone back to the old natural ways of farming their enclosed properties; living side by side, they'd worked out something between them. Billet surmised that perhaps whatever had gone haywire, VSU called in Allendale to assist them.

Another inhuman bawl reverberated across the countryside.

Squatting beside the man, LaFleur grimaced in pain as Butkus responded to the awful emission by grabbing one of his thick arms. He gripped it so tightly, his fingers dug into Lucius's arm.

"We gotta get the hell out of here before that thing comes back," Butkus said, sounding like a man who had dropped off into the deep end and was afraid to crawl his way back out.

"I think I see something out there," Mulholland said from his vantage point on the other side of the culvert.

An old, overgrown golf course sprawled along the northwestern property of the expansive VSU campus. Though afar, a few sparse trees blocked a clear view, Billet thought he saw something *big* moving on the other side of the mogul-humped greens.

A group of Reganites from the transport were checking

another small pickup truck sitting on its side. With a heave, they rocked it, tipping it back right side up under a protest of abused springs and metal.

"Does that thing run?" Billet called, keeping a sidelong glance to the spot in the distance. Whatever it was, it moved beyond a hill and some trees. He thought he could still see a small sliver of it even above the hillock.

One of the men struggled with the driver's side door, yanking it open. He grimaced. Billet could hear him mumble something about blood, and then the man checked inside. He slid in, looked to be tinkering with something, then the truck started up. Another man gave Jake the thumbs up.

Billet looked at LaFleur. "I want you out of here. Load your guys up and go like the devil himself is chasing you."

Lucius looked at him. "You can't expect to fight that thing on your own."

"Who said anything about fighting," Jake replied. "If whatever they've unleashed has done even half of this carnage, I have no plans to confront it."

LaFleur looked at his men, looked at Butkus who stared off to some other planet.

"Put him in the back of the pickup," Lucius said pointing at Butkus then to the pickup truck. "Let's get moving."

Mulholland trotted up out of the culvert and hurried to the back of the Huron. He and another man dragged a crate of meat. The gunner looked at Billet for a nod of approval. Jake gave it.

"If we run into another group of ferals, we're going to be in serious trouble," he said to himself.

Billet shook the big man's hand. The other Reganites followed suit, shaking hands and wishing them luck.

"You Gurks ain't so bad," one of the men said as he shook Billet heartily.

"Make sure you tell folks back home," Jake said referring to

Reganshire. "I know Silas isn't partial to Grand Rapids, but I'd rather work with you than against you these days."

He meant it, but knew you couldn't change a staunch old man and his fucked up offspring. A fleeting image of Rebecca Regan made him shiver.

"Let's go, folks," Billet said climbing back up to the transport's rooftop.

Phelps gunned the twin diesels.

Stokes, still at his post, looked southward towards where the thing had last been seen. He held the grips of his quad MG's, ready to fire.

"My spider senses are tingling, Captain. I don't like this one bit," the gunner said.

"Ease off the triggers, Sergeant, and save the tingling for the ladies back home," Billet said. "We ain't going near whatever's out there."

Billet watched the Reganshire LTV and the pickup dart off in the direction they'd just came. The Huron slowly started moving forward.

"What if *that* isn't its plan?" Stokes mumbled.

"Captain!" Lettner's voice called from beneath Billet inside the transport.

Rolling his eyes, Jake slipped back down inside the carrier. He found the holier-than-thou regent not strapped in and standing near one of the skinny rectangular side view ports.

"Have I not told you to strap in?" Jake said putting a hand to the ceiling as the vehicle bounced over something.

"You're letting those, those men drive away?" Lettner blustered, pointing towards the rear of the Huron as if he could stab the departing Reganites with his finger. "That gorilla friend of yours knows who I am. They've made me, know who I am, and will surely send someone to intercept us.

"You heard what he said about Silas Regan," Lettner

continued. "They got a whole army out to prevent me from getting home. Hell, for all I know they were the group who shot down my helicopter. We were just about over their territory when…"

"They probably did," Jake replied back. Intel said it was, but he didn't want to add fuel to the man's fire. "By the time that ragtag bunch returns to town, if something else doesn't accost them on the way, we'll have so much distance ahead of them, they'd never catch up.

"Whatcha worried about? Old man Regan catching you and nailin' you for murdering his brother?" Jake knew he pushed buttons he shouldn't but he had about enough of the man. He didn't go where he really wanted to fearing he'd lose control.

"How dare you!" The regent fumed, balling his fists. "There hasn't ever been any proof I'd anything to do with the Muskgeon Under-Commissioner's death, nor the other council members who were lost in that convoy."

Billet forced himself to bite back telling the man he hadn't brought up the others in the regent's council. He held back from delving into the mysterious circumstances that led to a large group of Lettner's constituents meeting a grisly demise. They'd been en route along the very road they now traveled on the day Lettner ordered the bio-chemical dump that cleansed the lakeshore lands of both unliving and living.

A vision of Jake's wife and son bathed in the yellow chemical wash, screaming as their flesh boiled away, flooded his mind. He hadn't been there, but knew what Lettner's purging "bath" did.

He felt his control leeching away.

He was suddenly in Lettner's face with fists full of the regent's flak jacket.

"I am telling you for the last time, sit your ass down or I'll throw you out and you'll be walking home from here!"

Murder was in his eyes and Lettner knew it. For a moment, the regent remained silent, and appeared almost fearful.

Then he gritted his teeth and pushed Billet away from him. "Get your hands off me. Grand Rapids and its citizenry aren't any better than those bloody heathens of Reganshire."

Jake knew Lettner meant to say *he* wasn't any better than the lot of Reganites. He cocked back his fist and...

"Captain, we got trouble," Phelps called in his ear bud.

Billet turned and took the three steps to the cab door, pulling it open to talk directly to the woman.

"Should have just gone and cleansed you all," Jake heard Lettner mumble as he shoved his head into the driver's cab.

Phelps peered out the small viewport to her left as she white-knuckled the steering yoke and slowly matted the accelerator.

Through the same viewport, Billet didn't have to ask her what the trouble was as he looked over her shoulder. The blood drained from his face. His heart did a high dive into his gut.

"Saint Michael protect us," Loutonia whispered.

Billet watched as assured doom raced towards them.

"We might need more than that," he added.

CHAPTER SEVEN
The Doom Bull and the Dead Men

Like a speeding semi-truck, and equally the size of one, a beast genetically altered for God knows what reason, and bent on trampling humankind to a bloody smear bore down on the Huron.

Billet struggled to keep his footing as he rushed from the cab, back to his topside hatch. The vehicle suddenly veered right. Jake grabbed the footing of the cupola, grimacing when his chest struck the steel ribbing.

Not buckled in, he watched as Lettner went face first into the bulkhead.

Stokes and Mulholland were already firing at the creature as he climbed to his perch. He ducked as Stokes swung the quads in his direction, nearly taking his head off. Jake opened his mouth to chastise the gunner, almost biting through his tongue as the transport snapped to the left, avoiding an overturned car in the middle of the road.

"Gawddamn, gawddamn, gawddamn!" Stokes swore aloud.

God had nothing to do with it. Billet held the hatch ring in a death grip and looked at the monster chasing them. It turned through the intersection at 48th Avenue and M-45, following them in their westerly direction, crashing through a defunct fast food restaurant, blasting it to kindling without breaking stride.

Grown from a test tube or at one point a regular beast altered through warped science, the enormous bull appeared taller than the HTV and nearly as wide. Either from experimentation or simply grown too large for it, the creature's furry hide was non-existent. Red exposed muscle and tendon ran from head to hoof. Though thicker in the chest and shoulder regions, extra musculature wound round the hulking body. A red barb made up its bovine tail, ending in a few long colorless strands, more like knitting needles than hair. Its legs were massive steel I-beams wrapped in corded sinew.

"Phelps, keep her steady," Jake howled into his throat mike.

"If we wedge a car in a tread or bust an axle, we won't be moving at all," Phelps returned as she brought the transport over the grass-choked median, bringing the vehicle onto an eastbound lane that was less debris filled.

Billet watched the mutated bull close the distance between them. The beast's massive head was as red and fleshless as its body, a creature straight from Hell. A Longhorn variant, its goalpost-shaped horns were dark and stained with gore. It wore a crumpled car door, and a small section of crumbling wood and drywall off each horn along with a number of torn and twisted bodies. Skewered near the sharp tips, the bloody carcasses flopped; broken marionettes. Torn at the abdomen and nothing more than the waist remaining, one poor fellow's intestines flailed behind him like morbid streamers.

The gunners continued firing as the beast charged and ran parallel to the transport. Phelps wasn't pushing Huron to top speed, but damn close. She went back over the median as the creature leaned in to give the vehicle a nudge.

"No, you don't," she said over the comm.

A row of small trees met their demise as she crossed back into the westbound lane.

Billet saw the big dark eyeball of the thing peer at him as it easily followed them. The eye, big as Jake's head, gazed at him, into him, so full of malice it froze every muscle in Billet's body. He was human. He'd known fear, but this thing appeared it wouldn't be done even if it killed him six ways from Sunday.

"I hate college mascots," Stokes said over the roar of the machine guns.

Jake drew his pistol as the giant bull veered in to ram them. He fired at the eye; what looked to be the only soft target on the massive skull. He swore as he leaned away, the right horn of the beast looming an easy arms-length away. He swore at the dead man impaled and dangling off the tip of the horn. He wasn't dead but undead, clawing and hissing at Billet as it swung by.

The bull crossed in front of the Huron and moved in to start battering the right side of the vehicle.

"Keep pouring it on. Don't let it get in close," Billet yelled as his gunners peppered the creature with hot lead. "I'm not sure we could sustain a direct hit from that thing."

He'd seen enough cars and good sized trucks toppled and flipped in their vicinity. They were much larger and heavier, but again, so was the gigantic brute buzzing them like an angry bee.

"Here it comes," Stokes shouted, pouring every round from his blazing gun barrels into the thing's skinless cranium.

The bullets bounced off the thick skull though red, oozing bits chipped off and spun away. Two bodies dangled off its left horn. The headless, limbless cadaver gutted at the bend in the massive horn wore tattered remains of a blue lab coat. Impaled near the tip of the horn, the other body, this one a white-eyed ghoul of a thing, a Feral, lived on, snarling and scraping the air. Stokes could understand its anger, speared in a manner that made the gunner's own rectum clench.

The bull raged in, slamming its bulk against the side of the transport, nearly bringing the passenger side wheels and track off the ground. The awful horn with the two dangling bodies swung in line with Stoke's gun position. He fired until it appeared he might be the next victim skewered.

Unable to angle his guns further, Stoke's leaned away as the zomb on horn tip got close enough to touch him. With a blood-dirty, emaciated foot—which flopped loosely, twisted opposite of how a foot should be aligned—the pierced Feral kicked the gunner in the side of the head. It followed up with raking claws, shrieking like a banshee through shredded vocal cords.

Billet saw the usually unyielding gunner start to crumple as Stokes' head rang off his hatch coaming.

As if trying to push the vehicle sidelong, the bull remained leaning against the Huron, keeping gait with it. The rotter bobbed like a puppet on a string, an evil sneer on the portion of its damaged face that still offered expression. The horn dipped in again, bringing another opportunity for the undead vermin to peel the helpless gunner's flesh.

Jake started to climb from his cupola to intercede, knowing he would be too late. He fell back as a single sizzling shot took the zomb's putrid head from its shoulders. Another perfectly placed, bone-shattering round clipped the upper haft of the horn, sending the headless rotter somersaulting down and away.

"Nice shootin'," Billet nodded at Mulholland.

Mulholland nodded back and continued stinging the beast with bullets.

"I had that," Stokes said pulling himself back upright using the weapons grips to do so. "You don't have to steal my thunder."

The gunner fired off a salvo as the beast slowed and let the transport move ahead of it. The gun fire flew wide without touching the creature. What used to be a small drive-thru coffee shop on the north side of the road took the brunt, the machine gun fire blowing out what was left of its dusty front windows.

"You all right, soldier?" Jake asked.

"I'm fine. Thing didn't even touch me," Stokes replied, though the pale expression on his face said different.

"Yeah, he always shoots like that," Mulholland commented over the comm.

"If that thing has dented or dinged my rig, I'm gonna be mad," Phelps said breaking in.

Jake ducked down to peer back inside the transport. The regent sat buckled in now. He glanced up at Billet. If looks could kill.

"This is why this place needs to be dusted," Lettner said.

Billet had no time to reply as Stokes yelled, nearly popping his eardrums, "It's comin' back around!"

Jake hardly lifted himself topside when the Huron jerked to the right, diesel engines revving. The heavy rear treads chewed up pavement, flinging chunks of asphalt high into the air.

"Gawddang, Phelps, y-you're gonna drain the fuel tanks b-before we get out of h-here," Mulholland said over the comm, teeth chattering. Billet could see both gunners hanging on for dear life.

The horned mutilation bore down on them. Its massive head angled in with chin at its bulky chest. Billet wasn't sure what a head on collision would bring, but several tons of animal meeting several tons of steel could not be good for him and his crew.

"Phelps!" he yelled in the comm.

The transport veered left at the last minute, though the bull hit and caromed the right side of the Huron. The sidelong graze brought the wheels and rear treads off the pavement and contorted the men violently in their cupolas. A series of vertebrae popped while Jake fought to keep himself boots down on his stand.

Billet watched the beast turn, its speed causing it to swing wide, disappearing into a row of houses on the opposite side of the street. Splintering wood and debris rose in the creature's wake. Jake hoped there were no squatters residing in the old homes, as the majority of the small community of farmers and property owners maintained places centrally located further west.

"We need to corral this thing and steer it away from Allendale," Billet said, pivoting around to keep eyes behind them.

"How do you corral… hell, even control, something that big," Stokes replied, swiveling his guns rearward, as did Mulholland.

The bull galloped back out into the main roadway, rubble rolling like smoke off its red hide. It lunged forward, its exposed massive leg muscles pumping.

"It's gonna ride right up our ass," Mulholland said in a panic.

"Hold your fire until its a few car lengths away," Jake said, sweat rolling down his brow, cool in the breeze of the fast moving vehicle.

In four long strides the bull drew nearly on top of them. Mulholland and Stokes fired. Great chunks of thick flesh sluiced off from the huge cranium, wide shoulders and chest of the mutated creature.

It did not faze it.

Like a steam engine belching, it snorted through flared nostrils big as manhole covers. The monster rammed the rear of the Huron. Phelps cursed through the comm, doing her best to bring the vehicle under control as the violent and solid shove threatened to tip them sideways. The bull broke away under the squealing of front tires and blur of smoking rubber.

"I think that oversized piece of hamburger scratched my baby," Loutonia said, breaking from her series of swearing. "That thing hurt my baby."

Billet flinched as Stokes fired a round from the 40mm auto-cannon mounted within the bouquet of his quad MG's.

"Gawddamn it," Jake swore as the round missed the bull by a mile, blasting a huge smoking divot in someone's overgrown front yard.

"I thought it an emergency," Stokes said innocently, shrinking under Jake's glare.

Jake's annoyance blew out. The action gave him an idea.

"Phelps, let that thing get in front of us," Jake said. "Then I want you guns and cannon to keep the beast in line. We'll drive it, old school, out of town."

"Old school, sir?" Mulholland said through the earbud.

"You always wanted to be a cowboy when you were a little kid, didn't cha?" Billet said watching the bull swing out under full gallop, turning a small house and adjoining garage into kindling before starting its return trip.

A second of silence, and then Mulholland replied: "Umm, not really, sir."

"We're coming up on the Allendale enclosure," Phelps reminded Jake.

Billet looked ahead seeing the gatehouse and a small group of Allendale militia standing at the ready.

"We'll have to go through it and hopefully keep ourselves and the creature on the roadway," Jake said, seeing no other options. If they veered off course now, they'd take the thing on a diagonal path through the "residential" part of town. He had no idea how many civilians were along that route and didn't want to bring the thing raging down upon innocent heads.

"Aren't they going to have an issue with that?" Phelps commented.

"If we let it run wild, there might not be anyone left to repair what little damage we end up doing," Jake replied.

Allendale could bitch back to Grand Rapids and the GRCC. Billet didn't care. He was already in the frying pan on high heat.

The giant creature came again at the transport. It angled its monstrous head, the horns coming in to skewer it.

Phelps hit the brakes, throwing Jake into the rim of the hatch and causing Mulholland and Stokes to howl in surprise and anger. The bull shot by the front end of the Huron, correcting itself and running out in front as the cursing driver throttled up.

"Not this time, fella," Phelps said.

"Get Allendales' attention." Billet steadied himself and looked ahead at the entry gate to the fast-approaching village. "Signal them to get the hell out of there. Flash 'em your high beams," he said to Phelps.

"Now that's what I'm talking about," Stokes added in.

Jake shot the lecherously grinning gunner a sour look.

"You're gonna have to open your mouth to scratch your balls if you keep that up, mister," Phelps said through the comm.

"Promises, promises," Stokes replied, chuckling unconvinced.

Jake couldn't tell if Loutonia flashed the oncoming gatehouse the warning lights, but the group of armed men at the gate suddenly separated and went for opposite sides of the enclosure.

They were upon the place in a heartbeat. The bull crashed through the wood and thin steel barricade like a child smashing through a Tinker toy set.

"Aim well, men. No civilian casualties. No home or building demolition." He knew Stokes looked at him to see if the statement was geared towards him. Jake kept his eyes focused ahead.

No more than a semi-truck length ahead of them, the massive bull tried to stray from the roadway. It veered left. An explosion of asphalt erupted on the left, turning the creature to the right. It veered right. A curbed section of concrete, a portion of grassy street-side berm and a small tree disappeared in a gout of flame and smoke, turning the beast back to center of road.

They sped on, nearing the center of the small village. On the right loomed a large tan building which had been a high school. It was now a combination hospital and living center for all ages. Stacked rolls of concertina wire lined the perimeter of the building grounds, stretching nearly its entire two block length. Small sheds stood every 30 yards or so along the razor wire fencing; guard shacks with sufficiently armed men and women standing close by. People stood in the doorways of the building while the militia scurried up and down the lot out front.

"Jeezuz, if the things out for blood, they might as well all wave and cheer at it," Phelps said as they continued their pursuit, explosions and machine gun fire pounding the ground on either side of the giant creature as they went.

"Maybe they ain't scared of it," Stokes said as a plume of smoke rolled over them.

Billet squinted as the air cleared. He opened his mouth to exclaim his surprise when the 120mm turret cannon of the Abrams tank spoke for him, spitting out its own explosive payload at the passing monstrosity.

The beast jerked sideways but did not fall as its mountainous right shoulder exploded from the shell impact. A cloud of foul blood and viscera blew back against the HTV, washing over it like chunky red rain. Jake survived the brunt of it, turning his stand so the heavy hatch shielded him. Stokes took it straight in the face, cursing through the wave. Having a chance to see it coming, Mulholland ducked beneath the lip of his cupola, avoiding the warm offal.

"Where'd they get the armor?" Phelps said over the comm.

"That'll be on *my* report," Jake responded, borrowing the infamous term from the piece of shit inside the transport below him.

If they make it back.

He watched the rear end of the massive bull grow as the Huron rushed up upon it. Phelps and Stokes shouted in unison as the animal, slowed by the shot from the Abrams, let the transport catch up. The carrier jerked as the brakes were applied, but not before the rear section of the bull met the front end of the vehicle.

Billet felt his vertebrae snap in the other direction as he was thrown forward. He ducked as the creature's stumpy red tail lashed across the face of the Huron. The coarse, sparse hairs raked the metal body of the transport like steel barbs.

"Big cow ass," Stokes growled as he opened fire again, back to his quad MG's. The hail of bullets bit harmlessly as before, and the gunner cursed more as a fresh rain of the beast's crimson essence dowsed him.

"If you are referring to me..." Phelps snarled into everyone's earbud.

"Gawddamnit! Eyes on target, people!" Jake bellowed.

They made the western end of the Allendale Hospital-residential building with the Abrams and running, firing militia in close pursuit.

Billet swore aloud as the big tank fired again, throwing a shot under the beast and to the left. It was *way* too close for comfort with the HTV halfway up the thing's ass. Jake wondered if the fine folks of AMA (Allendale Municipality Authority) were also firing at the GRCC. He felt a sudden flush of guilt bringing it through their doorway. You ask for what you get sometimes.

"Captain, they are trying to make radio contact," Phelps said.

"I think they've already made themselves very clear." Jake glanced towards the small army on the opposite side of the razor wire enclosure. "Let's move this thing outta town," he said as Phelps slowed enough to let the bull get a few lengths ahead of them again.

"Cannon again, sir?" Mulholland asked, almost giddy.

"Affirmative, just like before, gents. Keep the patterns tight."

"*I* can do *that*, sir," the rear gunner added. Jake knew the statement directed at the Lance Corporal's counterpart at the other gun station.

Stokes threw an arm up behind himself, and flipped off *his* counterpart.

With the giant bull ahead of them, and the cannon fire keeping it in line, they sped by the western gate of the hospital compound. Hanging out of a pickup truck with the Allendale Engine House No. 5 emblem on the door, Billet watched a man in a red beret wag an angry finger at two men at the tall, barbed exit gate. The two guardsmen appeared to struggle with opening it to let the traffic jam of local troops out. Not knowing the intentions of the rousted town, Jake was relieved with the malfunction.

The bull bawled angrily as it tried to run outside the plumes of blasted roadbed and explosions. A double tap from Stoke's cannon turned the beast wide and to the right as they got to the intersection of M-45 and 68th Avenue. A string of guardsmen at the gate only held weapons on the creature for a nanosecond before thinking better of it. They avoided going back inside the old gas station building on the southeast corner of the intersection, fortunately, as the bull crashed through it, still at full gallop. Stokes punctuated the damage by a shot which brought the roof down. The beast blasted through the outer perimeter fencing and the transport followed suit.

"Damn thing dented my baby," Phelps hissed. "But I'm going to run out of fuel if we keep this up."

Already she started to slow the Huron. Mulholland and Stokes continued the firing with Billet throwing lead at the thing's back side. They passed the old granary and feed store, and The Meat Market. Jake briefly grunted in mirth at the coincidental absurdity of it, including at the men who ran out with rifles and pistols drawn, as the bull and HTV roared by.

"Save something for getting us out of here and to the LZ."

"Yessir," she replied.

"Hold your fire," Jake said as he watched the huge creature run further ahead.

Mulholland fired a shot keeping the brute from turning west, and, in full gallop, the beast continued northbound along 68th avenue without further prodding.

Billet pumped a fist in the air, rejoicing at the small victory.

"Let Eastmanville and Coopersville deal with it," Stokes said, turning to Billet.

Shit, Jake internalized.

Phelps took them off 68th, turning west on Pingree. It was all open fields and farmland as far as the eye could see.

"Get us back out onto 45," Billet said, feeling the adrenaline rush start to leech away. He felt suddenly very tired. "Let's get this thing over with."

Wiping the grit and bloody grime as best he could from himself, with a heavy sigh, Jake slowly descended down into the bowels of the transport. He hoped perhaps the regent had met his demise somehow during the fighting, but knew it couldn't be a reality.

"Trying to fucking kill me?" William Lettner spat as Billet dropped into the hold.

CHAPTER EIGHT
All Our Dead Belong To Us

"**A**s we get close to the end here, I need to tell you, it's been a pleasure," Lettner said leaning back in his seat, arms folded sternly across his chest. His calm expression turned into a hateful sneer as he continued. "It has been a pleasure seeing what an absolute shithole West Michigan has become.

"Grand Rapids is run by a bunch of buffoons who could care less for their people, letting a populace of rotting, useless fleshbags remain in their midst... hell, supporting a populace of those disgusting creatures. Feeling empathy for these monsters only because they might have been family or friends, living viable citizens," Lettner said grimacing as if tasting something sour and foul while he spoke.

"I will get my way. Mark my words," the regent warned, waving a finger at Jake. "Mark my words. If and when I find the chance, and I can guarantee you there will be a *when*, I will come in and cleanse that city, her surrounding neighborhoods and lands, including those Neanderthals of Reganshire, and whatever man and beast still roam that university campus..."

He took a breath, gritting his teeth, brows so drawn his eyes were dark caves under the furrowed ledges. He clenched his fists, visibly trembling with rage.

He exhaled, "I...will...cleanse this entire place...and make it my own."

The Regent of Muskegon fumed and looked ready to explode. If he had the means at the moment, he would have surely wiped the perceived dark blemish off the face of West Michigan.

The flame blew out when, finally having all of the man he could stand, Billet smashed his palm into the emergency release on the seat pan belt. Eyes bulging, Lettner wheezed as he was taken by vest, shirt and a pinch of skin underneath, and violently jerked from his seat.

Catching his breath, Lettner went to protest. Billet punched him in the jaw, staggering him so all the man could do was stumble along as Jake dragged him towards the rear of the transport.

"Captain?" Loutonia asked, standing in the cab doorway as Jake hit the rear door hatch release.

Her look of extreme concern did not slow Jake's determined gait.

"What are you going to do, sir?" Mulholland said stepping down from his perch. "We've come this far. Is this going to jeopardize the mission?"

As the rear hatch dropped with a metallic squeal, Billet gave the regent a shake to snap him out of his stupor. He wanted the man coherent.

As the waning daylight flooded the inside of the carrier, Jake turned and looked at his distraught gunner. His eyes went to the young soldier, to Phelps, to Stokes. It was the first time in a bad situation the squat gunner wasn't throwing in a line of sarcasm. Jake's rage did not abate as he peered at his worried crew.

"I'm taking this sonuvabitch outside to show him the error of his ways. I'll only be..." he drew his pistol, "...a moment."

Lettner struggled to break from Jake's steely grip, peering

back at the silent crew.

"Do something! Are you idiots just going to stand there?" The regent bellowed.

Mulholland, Stokes and Phelps looked at each other.

"I'm calling our pick-up." Phelps said as Billet dragged his cursing cargo outside.

***

Through a dry, overgrown drainage ditch, to an equally overgrown but still discernible two track pathway, Billet pulled Lettner. When the regent was about to get his legs underneath him, Jake yanked, keeping the man in a constant off-balance stumble. They walked along the weed-choked path, patches of gravel showing up here and there. It had been an unpaved driveway at one time.

Jake kept his eyes to the dense tree line a hundred yards off to his west and the tall, flat grassy field to the east. Though he hadn't visited since last year, on the fourth anniversary of his wife and son's death, the wilds could change, and with the Ferals and the giant bull incident, he wasn't going to drop his guard while outside the HTV. One of the reasons for the drawn sidearm, though he would continue to let the regent sweat it out. Tempting, but...

"Do you know where you are?" Billet said as he stopped halfway along the old driveway. He gave Lettner one last jerk and let him stand on his own two feet.

Another twenty yards to the south, an old farmhouse stood. The upper floor windows were shuttered except where some drooped on rusty hinges; the glass panes broken, the eyes of the house dark. The ground floor openings were boarded. The house had been white, but exposure to the elements gave it a rotted texture, much like the undead which had prevalently roamed the area before the cleansing. Grass and weeds grew to knee level and taller. A row of arborvitaes created a natural barricade along the front edges of the yard, though they bulged monstrously, years since they'd seen a good shearing.

Lettner rubbed the area of his jaw where Billet's fist had landed, and eyed the old house suspiciously.

"I know we are in West Olive Township." His eyes scanned the house and surrounding area. His eyes brightened, and then darkened as a sinister sneer crossed his countenance. "And before a crumbling old home that should have been torn down years ago."

Jake snarled and grabbed the regent by the neck and hauled him further along the drive, moving into the overgrown yard.

A fine yellowish dust curled off the grass and ground as they walked. The wild lawn wasn't exactly green, nor even the emerald branches of the trees and bushes both close and afar in the surrounding woodland. A subtle ochre hue tinged everything, outlining the waving blades of grass and the leaves in the trees that all drooped as if they held some faint sickness they could not discharge.

Nearly five years since Lettner had issued the orders to "dust" the west shoreline to eradicate the zombie blight, yet a faint wisp of the bio-chemical agent still clung to the region.

"You *know* where we're at?" Billet said as he pulled at Lettner, again offsetting the man.

Lettner coughed, struggling to regain his footing. "Of course, I know where we are, unless you enjoy showing me condemned homes for the undead."

With a shove, Billet let loose of the sharp-tongued regent. The man went down on his hands and knees, cursing as he quickly got back to his feet.

"I'd recommend you cease with this rough play, Captain," Lettner warned, rubbing his neck. His cheek stood red and swollen, and he gingerly touched it when he was done with his neck.

Billet bit back what he really wanted to say about "playing" and instead: "Do you know why we're here?"

"I haven't a clue, and don't necessarily care," Lettner replied.

"I'm a bit more concerned with missing my real ride home."

"Over here," Jake said, waving the man around the side of the house, using his pistol hand to do so. "I want to show you what your lack of caring does."

On the east side of the house, a shed-sized greenhouse stood. A flowerbed framed the perimeter of the small out-building, withered rose bushes set at all four corners. The thick plate glass windows were glazed over with dirt and grime. A glass tile from the four-pane roof lay broken inside the structure. A single bloody handprint, long dried and starting to fade, and a series of scratch marks rimmed the lower section of the glass shed. Other than that, all appeared more or less untouched.

The two men stopped before the shed; Billet purposely pushed Lettner so the man's face was up to the bolted and padlocked glass door.

"What do you see?" Jake said giving the man's neck a painful squeeze.

Lettner swore and peered inside.

Beyond the dirt-fogged glass, he saw light olive-green grass as if it hadn't quite seen enough sun. The only two items within the interior, lying side by side, oblong in the dull grass, were two headstones. Lettner could just read the larger lettering chiseled into the left grave marker: *Jenna rop-Billet*, the last name obscured by a clump of ashen moss running along the top edge of the stone. The other stone read: Joseph Billet.

The regent glanced back at the other headstone. "I hate when women have to have their maiden name in there."

Jake replied with his fist.

William Lettner found himself on the ground, spitting blood. He shook his head, clearing the swirling black path of unconsciousness trying to suck him down. Wiping the red spittle from his lips, he kicked out to keep the insane soldier off him.

Jake stepped back, the kick just grazing his shin. But his

boot heel knocked against a weed-hidden rock, and he stumbled backwards. Unbalanced, he went down on his backside. His sidearm dropped from his hand, landing an arms-length away. He was surprised at the other man's speed, knocked half-silly as he'd been, as the enraged regent launched himself, landing on top of him.

Jake accepted the blow to the jaw he received from Lettner. Glad the man showed some spirit. However, one was enough and he caught the man's left as it swung to hit him again.

"Wife and child," Billet said into the angry eyes of the man atop him. Lettner's right eye was starting to swell and blacken. "Wife and child, innocents you killed; two of the thousand plus who still lived in the area when you dowsed them with your dirty bomb."

"We called everyone to tell them to evacuate the area," Lettner said with mock concern. "Your line must have been disconnected."

In the blink of an eye, a mental image formed. Jake was not there but across state when the incident occurred. His wife and child died alone, leaving him burdened with the guilt and a feeling of failing he could never shake. He relied on the Intel from the first responders, and with that: he saw them.

He saw Jenna and Joey, Joe—at 19, he hated being called that—huddled together in the front yard as the big C-130 flew over and vomited its contents upon the land. Jake saw the dull yellow rain fall, the flora bending unharmed by its pounding force, and the fauna—animal and man—literally melt against the flesh-dissolving liquid onslaught. He could hear their screams as skin and sinew drooled away to slick the ground crimson.

As the lakeshore cleansing consumed its zombie infestation, so were its helpless living populace obliterated.

And all under direction of the despotic rule of NSC Grand Muskegon High Councilman William Lettner, unopposed as he had sent his opposing peers on a death-assured trip through the same region on that same horrible day.

Jake kicked up, connecting with the regent's backside. He grabbed the man as he came forward, and flipped him over head to land on his back behind him.

Lettner didn't miss the chance during his tumble, snatching up the fallen pistol as he somersaulted to his feet.

The two faced each other in an instant.

"The deed needed to be done," Lettner snarled, gun aimed at Billet, "for the survival of our land and people. I have secured the lakeshore, and at some point, I will work my way inland and secure all West Michigan. The people will hail me, and the dead will stay dead."

"The dead will be more of us, more of the people who oppose you, who do not believe we need to simply eradicate these unfortunates who have not found peace in true death," Jake said, watching Lettner's trigger finger tense. "You know scientists right now are working on a cure for the virus. And rest assured, when the time comes, we'll all be able to 'move on' like we should."

Lettner huffed. "Like the mad men of VSU. You can see where that got them."

In the distance, the sharp chop of helicopter blades slapping the air could be heard.

"I think your head wound," the regent said waving the gun towards Jake's forehead, "has unsettled your mind. But again, I am thinking it's been unsettled for quite some time. I am surprised you, of all men, would've taken on a mission knowing you were transporting a man you held such animosity for."

"Captain, are you all ri…" Phelps said as she and Mulholland came running around the side of the house. They stopped in their tracks when they saw the scene before them.

Overhead, the sound of a helicopter drew closer.

Billet grinned, the action not missed by the Muskegon man.

"Your career is over. You and your crew," Lettner said,

confidence building as a massive tiltrotor V-22 Osprey came over the western tree line bearing the Wave-and-Sunset NSC emblem on its underside and ribbing. "I am arresting you for crimes against me and the lakeshore coalition."

Jake put his hands up, nodding to his driver and gunner to do the same. With the regent pointing a gun at their backs, they moved around to the front of the house where the Osprey set down between them and the roadside HTV.

Manning his quads like a good soldier, Stokes swiveled the guns towards the group as they came into view. Billet signaled him to stand down before the man accidentally bathed them under a hot lead shower.

The group stopped and shielded their faces as a swirl of grass and dirt whipped up under the chop of the aircraft as it touched down.

"I can use a vehicle like the Huron in my arsenal," Lettner said nodding towards the HTV as the Osprey's side doors slid open.

Billet remained grinning and silent.

Armed men in full battle dress spilled from the Osprey, the same Wave-and-Sunset badges and American Flag emblems on their sleeves. They fanned out around the aircraft, securing the area in case the...unsavory and undead...were in the general locale.

"My ride home," Lettner said.

A balding man in a black suit, same emblem on his suit jacket pocket, stepped out behind his troops. He came forward, rubbing a very thick but neatly trimmed mustache. He was accompanied by two guardsmen who stood taller than his own imposing figure. His dark, tired right eye—the other eye and side of his face horribly scarred from old chemical burns—grew bright with fury as his gaze fell upon the regent.

Lettner fell suddenly silent, too stunned to emit words.

"Hello, son. Trouble here?" The suited man said to Billet, saluting him stiffly, revealing his prosthetic left hand.

Transport

"No trouble, sir," Jake spun about and yanked his sidearm from the slack fingers of the agape Lettner. "Just visiting your daughter and grandson."

Billet pushed the regent out in front of him, the gun trained on *his* back now.

A gloomy expression passed over the tall man's ravaged face as his eye went momentarily to the side of the old house. "You can call me Zachariah," the man said returning to Billet. He looked to the befuddled and suddenly withered regent. "And you... you can call me *Mister* Holtrop, the recently sworn-in Grand Councilman of the North Shore Coalition."

"What...? You...?" Lettner blubbered, as the two towering guardsmen stepped around Holtrop and secured the fuming man. "You are supposed to be dead. The convoy...? You...?"

"As a famous and great American author once said, 'The reports of my death are greatly exaggerated.'" Holtrop grinned dangerously, the melted side of his face contorting in a monstrously malevolent pall.

Without the bushy mane of hair, Billet realized his ex-father-in-law looked much like the ancient writer he quoted.

"What trickery is this, Holtrop? I saw you come back in a body bag like all the others," Lettner fumed, struggling against his guards.

One of the restraining guards, *Campbell* on his name patch, looked ready to clock the struggling regent if he didn't simmer down.

"Not all your loyalists were loyal. Most were simply scared of you." Holtrop said, his gaze far away. "Being last in the convoy was a blessing in some regard. Councilwoman Mason is a paraplegic, and if it wasn't for my secretary shielding me when our car overturned, I might have actually been in that body bag."

The color drained from Lettner's face.

"For crimes against humanity, both living and...unliving, William Lettner, you are under arrest and will be tried immediately upon return to Muskegon by a jury of your peers," the new regent said, ominous as a dark tomb.

"What if I do not return to Muskegon? What if I request sanctuary in Grand Rapids?" Lettner said with all the confidence as if someone in the world still loved him.

"The surviving NSC council members and the mayor of Grand Rapids collaborated on this. You will find no sanctuary there." Holtrop exclaimed, rubbing his prosthetic hand with his real one as if it might bring feeling to the fake limb. "You might find some sympathy from the GRCC as a protocol or two were deviated to get you here."

Billet spat, his GRCC response.

Holtrop nodded. "It's time, William," he simply said.

"You!" Lettner pointed at Billet. The guards yanked back to keep the angry regent restrained. "You knew about this since we left. The gall! And you claim a call to honor and to safeguard all citizens."

Jake saw Lettner casting his poisonous gaze at Phelps and Mulholland.

"Only me and another crew member knew of the real mission," Jake snapped back. His hands were at his sides; his right on the grip of the pistol he'd just holstered. "As far as honoring and protecting all citizens; that *is* what I have done."

Lettner turned red as a beet. Jake expected flames and smoke to come pouring out of the enraged man.

Holtrop stepped up and handed Jake a thick leather pouch. "You and your crew earned this. Every cent." he said as Billet took the packet.

"I still know people. I will see you discharged," Lettner raged at Billet. "I'll remember you! You'll get yours!"

"This is for my crew," Jake said gripping the packet, turning and handing it to Phelps who handed it to Mulholland. They both looked at Billet with a queer questioning look on their face.

"This…" Jake said, pulling his pistol from holster. "…is for me."

No one had time to react. If the Muskegon guards had been focused, Jake surely would have been lying in a pool of blood before he could squeeze the trigger. Instead, everyone ducked, flinched, or leaned away as two shots were fired from the gun. The guardsman securing Lettner's left arm let go as the slugs hit the *ex*-regent in the upper arm, blasting into bone and muscle. Crumpling, the man screamed as the guard tried to grab him by the same arm.

"Now you'll remember me," Billet said, re-holstering, and putting his hands up. The Muskegon militiamen surrounding the aircraft had their weapons suddenly trained on him.

Standing up from a partial crouch, Zachariah Holtrop looked to Lettner. A medic jumped from the Osprey to aid the cursing, wounded man. "That was a bit excessive, wasn't it?" Holtrop said, turning to Billet.

"He is lucky I held back this long," Jake said, waiting for further reprimand. The other man might be his father-in-law, but he was also the head man now for a circuit that Billet wasn't part of. Regardless of relation, Holtrop could throw the book at him if he so desired.

No further comment or action ensued.

The new regent signaled his men to mount up. Blades still slowly spinning began to come to life again as the big tiltrotor prepared for departure.

"You've done a good thing here, you and your crew," Holtrop said, offering his good hand to Billet.

Jake took it though the strong handshake did nothing to ease his troubled thoughts as he looked to the aircraft, knowing the foul cargo it held now.

Phelps and Mulholland saluted and thanked the Grand Councilman.

Zachariah looked at Jake. "Jenna and Joseph have been, will be, avenged," the older man said with a hand on Jake's shoulder. "All those the man thoughtlessly slaughtered will be avenged. His trial is in two days. The judge had relatives who lived out here. There isn't anyone who hasn't been affected by Lettner's actions. I can guarantee he'll hang post-verdict."

Jake gave the man a weak smile. He'd never done him wrong, and knew he had the gumption and ability to make things happen. Still, he wouldn't rest easy until he heard Lettner lay six feet under and *dead* dead. He wished he could be the one putting the final bullet through the man's brain to keep him from rising. Some other lucky bastard would get the honors.

"Sir," the guard named Campbell said rushing out to Holtrop. "We're ready to roll."

Holtrop nodded and the tall guard stood back, waiting to usher him onboard.

"The old cottage is not far from here. Haven't been there since last summer. It's locked down, but the code is still the same: Jenna's birth date. Go there for some R&R. You've earned it," the councilman said. "Fence is always on. Keeps the Z's and squatters away."

Mulholland and Phelps thanked the regent, and started back towards the Huron.

Jake nodded. "Thank you, sir."

The Muskegon councilman turned away, stopped, and looked back at Billet. "We are still related, Jacob. We have things cleared with Grand Rapids. Honeywell approved of the mission. Colonel Jackson might have you scrubbing toilets for a while, but…"

"Sir," Campbell called over the increasing chop of the Osprey.

"We'll surely be in need of you in Muskegon when shit hits the fan over Lettner. Always someone protesting for the wrong reasons, causing an uproar. I'm suspecting I'll get some flak too from the populace. You'll always have a place, son," Holtrop said as he started towards the aircraft.

Jake looked back at the house. He could see himself and his wife sitting on the front porch, watching their son play in the front yard. Holding hands, watching the sun drop over the western skyline, her slender hand warm in his. He could feel her against him, the old farmhouse's drafty chill keeping her close on those cold winter nights.

He saw Holtrop on the stoop of the Osprey's doorway. Jake saluted him. The councilman, his father-in-law, nodded and climbed aboard.

"Always have a place," Jake repeated in a small voice over the roar of the aircraft.

The Osprey lifted off. Stokes, Mulholland and Phelps stood at the transport, a blur in the haze of the dusty backwash.

With one last glance back at the house, Jake headed down the overgrown two-track towards the Huron.

***

The Holtrop cottage stood on a sandy bluff over Lake Michigan. Behind it, inland and across the road, the old Consumers Energy power plant and Pigeon Lake resided. Surrounded by pines and poplars, the small A-frame abode sat secluded from other homes and cottages along this section of West Michigan lakeshore. Covered over with the ever-shifting sand, the nearby township park lay silent and empty a stone's throw south. Though Jake visited the place many times with his wife and son, it seemed a forever ago since those times.

Inside the cottage, in the center of the small living room area, encircling a rickety coffee table, the cheap wood veneer flaking and peeling like dry skin, the crew of the Huron sat. Each with a bundle of cash courtesy of the NSC, they counted the pile of bills as a opened fifth of what appeared to be aged, expensive bourbon whiskey stood amidst the green backs.

"If I'd have known I could make this much in one haul, I would have signed up to take ten of those greedy bastards out on the road," Mulholland said with one hand grasping a wad of twenty-dollar bills and the other a shot glass of the amber liquid. He threw the contents of the shot glass down his throat, making his pronounced Adam's apple bob. He immediately turned green and looked as if he might paint the floor.

Stokes nodded, and slugged his bourbon from the large glass he held. He shivered violently as the antiquated, and obviously not so smooth, liquor hit his gut.

Her own shot glass spilling over, Phelps tipped her head back and quaffed her portion. She emitted a little cough, made a sour face, and set the glass down.

"Whoo! Only the dead or dying would enjoy this swill," she said and returned to the small stack, but large amount, of money before her. "This should take care of buffing up the body of my poor rig after that overgrown chunk of ground round dented her up."

Kicking his muddy boots up onto the coffee table, Stokes threw his thick hairy arms behind his head. He cast the woman's chest a lecherous look, and said, "Babe, if you buff up that body anymore…"

The man laughed and looked at Mulholland.

Mulholland did not react, knowing better, and inspected his glass as if he'd not heard his rude crew mate.

Loutonia ignored Stokes. She looked towards the screened balcony door leading out to a narrow wood deck. The deck perched over a sandy hill with a clear view of the shoreline and rolling waves of Lake Michigan. She stood and headed towards it.

"I can shoot him if you want," Mulholland said, joking.

Stokes flipped him the bird.

Not looking back, Phelps walked to the balcony slider.

***

Jake inhaled deeply, trying to take a cleansing breath. He clasped the deck railing, fingers poked by splinters from the seriously weather-abused wood. He leaned against the enclosure, peering out at the dark waters of the big lake and the star-dotted ebon above. A first quarter moon cast its light down on the roiling surf; it created a gently rippling silver line from the far horizon to the shore. A few months from now, the icy blanket of winter would fall across the region, freezing the shoreline solid and dusting it with thick white coldness.

"A hundred dollars for your thoughts, Captain?" Loutonia said stepping up beside him, assuming the same stance and far gaze out onto the lake.

Jake turned to Loutonia. "I know you have it, and I'd hate to unload all that's on my mind to make it worth all that cash. You might request a refund."

She shrugged, and he continued: "I think I am going to get a reaming by the brass for deviating from plan and putting a slug in Lettner when we get back to town. That job in Muskegon might be what we need until I know I'm not bringing you guys back to a firing squad or something."

He kid about the firing squad, though he was sure he'd get his ass gnawed good for taking the HTV off the planned route. He hadn't kept in communication with base, and did what he did even though the mission was a success: to bring into custody a man who threatened Grand Rapids and the whole west side of the state, and a murderer to boot. There's no hero's welcome when rules and protocol are broken even to save the world.

"Meh. I hear they need an armored escort for equipment and work crew bringing wind turbines from Wisconsin to New Holland," Loutonia said, trying to sound upbeat considering the dark mood emanating from her commander. "We can always do that if the fire remains hot around here. I already kind of signed us up," she finished slightly sheepishly, not sure how he'd react to her signing them up for a new task.

Jake smiled, almost cracking his stern face. "Always thinking ahead."

They grew quiet, both staring out at the dark lake, listening to the soft hush of the waves rolling up onto the shore.

"Thinking about them?" Phelps said referring to his wife and son.

"Always. Whenever I get close to this area. Yeah."

Jake jerked slightly but settled as his driver's cool hand slid into his and clasp it. Her dark skin eclipsed his under the shadow of the night.

"We can't ever forget them. I can't, and don't plan to," she said as her thoughts wisped over her own deceased children, and even her abusive, late ex-husband.

She moved closer to Jake, leaning warmly against him. "We can only keep moving forward, keep pushing forward, and hope what we do will let us join them when we are finished here."

Jake Billet shirked the heavy emotions teasing at his tired senses. He breathed out, relaxed, let the sound of the lake wash his dread thoughts away. He turned and tenderly kissed Loutonia's forehead, eyes to the interior of the cottage as he did so to make sure his other crew members didn't notice their affection.

Feeling his dark mood abating, he broke away from the woman, patting her hand before they stepped apart. "Let's get back inside. I need a drink and a hot shower," he said as he gestured her to go first.

"I would recommend avoiding your father-in-law's rotgut," Loutonia said as she opened the screen slider and headed inside.

Billet glanced off towards the front of the cottage; the Huron stood parked like its own massive outbuilding. All seemed quiet. He'd see it in the morning, another day to begin anew. *Good enough, he thought.*

"Phelps, I found a bathing suit owned by the missus. You could try it on and model for us," Jake heard Stokes say right before he stepped through the door. He saw the squat gunner grinning ear to ear, standing, holding up a woman's one piece bathing suit. Loutonia would *never* fit into it as his mother-in-law had been a wisp of a woman.

"Here we go," Mulholland said, gently sliding his chair back.

Loutonia glanced over her shoulder at Jake. "I am going to check on the rig one last time before I turn in."

She started towards the front door just off the living room, passing between Stokes and the cheap coffee table as the grinning little man stood, suit in hand, waggled brow and wagged his tongue. She spun on him. She kicked out, burying the toe of her boot deep into her crude crewmate's crotch.

"It's up," Mulholland responded.

Stokes rose a few inches off the floor, and then crashed down onto the coffee table, smashing it to splinters.

Loutonia continued on towards the front door.

"It's good!" Mulholland exclaimed raising his arms. Field goal!

Jake stepped in and closed the slider, expecting he'd have to break up the forthcoming fight...before Stokes got himself *really* hurt. He took a seat near the wreckage of both man and table, picking up the bottle of whiskey. Examining the label, he nodded approvingly, removed the cap and sniffed the contents.

Holding his bag of boot-crushed baubles, Stokes wheezed and squeaked, "I think I need to go to the hospital, Captain."

Jake raised the bottle to his lips, stopping before taking a pull. "Buck up, Sergeant. It's only your ego that's bruised," though he suspected Phelps had put some heart into it, "and that table."

Stokes groaned, curling into a fetal position.

"And the table is coming out of your pay," Jake continued, taking a long swig of the bourbon. "And if I find you've soiled that bathing suit..."

Stokes curled up tighter, swearing under his halting breath.

Jake took another draw from the bottle, and looked at the label admirably as he brought it to rest on his knee. The warmth of the liquor made him feel filled with the fire of life.

"Not bad. Not at all."

BILLET'S BITCH SESSION
Journal Entry - Wednesday, December 3, 2025

O kay. It's the holiday season, so I guess this will be more banter than bitching.

I had to excuse myself from our little poker game to take a call from Central Command. Probably not a bad thing to leave the game as Stokes was taking all our cash as usual. Poor Eddie, he can shoot the white out of a radish from a thousand yards, but can't play a hand of cards if he asked nicely.

I took the call in my room, feeling initially as frosty as the outside air. They have a good piling of snow here in Milwaukee. I guess across the big lake we're getting some major lake effect burying West Michigan, so I can't say if I'd rather be there at the moment.

Colonel Jackson was on the horn. I had spoken to him a little over a month ago after things settled down not only in Muskegon after Lettner's execution, but also after Intel got leaked on Mayor Honeywell's and the GRCC's intimate involvement in the whole thing. I always enjoy seeing my name in the newspaper. Groan.

Other than checking in on us (I think he is simply making sure we're not going to go AWOL on him) he informed me there are now threats from "loyalist groups"—misguided friends of the late NSC commissioner—sending nasty grams to Honeywell and the GRCC. Nothing major except someone tried to set fire to the JE Snell YMCA facility across the west side of the river. Dumbasses. Concrete walls don't burn. And I am sure the Gurks stationed there put some lead to the arsonists where the sun don't shine. If that's all the brains and bluster these Lettner enthusiasts got… Bring it!

The Colonel rambles on about some other things, politics amongst the Grand Rapids city council. Rupert Largo, the City Treasurer, is calling for Honeywell to resign. Blah blah blah. Fucking people. Death is right outside their door and they want to fight amongst each other.

I can't help it. My ears tune out, my mind on other things.

It's been a few months now since I made a scene at my old homestead, before my wife, my boy. I think about them, and that place. What it once was and now cannot ever be again, not with the land as it is, the world as it is, and definitely not with the memories.

But with those thoughts, I go even further back into that chest of reminiscences. Maybe I am getting tired of all this to be going back in my head to those years long ago. Going back to where I grew up, a few miles from downtown Grand Rapids, on the west side, before the bird flu-nudged blight, before the walls went up on the east side of the river, and the west side, my old childhood stomping ground, turned into a retention area for the cities undead folk.

I recall playing up in the woods, chestnut wars with friends as the evening sun cast the trees in long shadows. Laying on a big ole fallen tree, arms behind head, staring up into the blue sky, relaxing with no fears. Trips to the zoo, long before VSU bio-terrorists tainted the animals; walking along the Grand River out in the boonies, enjoying flora and fauna without worry of a feral group of rotters sneaking up and making a bloody dinner of you; seeing cars and a living populace fill the streets versus empty, weed-choked avenues, rusted-out metal husks, and walking carcasses.

Transport

I don't know why my mind slides off to those days of yore. They run thickly through my thoughts at the moment.

Maybe the season stirs a sliver of hope, and I hope we can change things and get things back to some form of normalcy. Maybe someday, some kid, like me back in the day, can enjoy life without all this insanity, can enjoy some simpler days and times.

The red lights blinking atop the twin smoke stacks of Wisconsin Electric Power towering above Interstate 94-43 catch my eye out of the south window. A spotlight from the heavily-guarded plant shines up at an area between the massive concrete pillars. Hung between the smoke stacks from the center catwalks are a half dozen Zees, and a couple thugs who travelled all the way from St. Paul just to get caught trying to loot some old downtown shops. The white light paints them all like ghosts, a stringer of dead frozen fish.

I re-focus on my reflection in the frosty glass. I look like a ghoul myself in all its pale scar-striped glory. The raised band of flesh across my forehead from the slash I took during the Lettner trip; real military Frankenstein monster appeal.

And both images outside and within, I realize, portray the future fairly clear.

The Colonel reels me back into reality with some Christmas well wishes to me and the crew, and to get my ass back to Michigan with his rig (Loutonia would've loved to heard that) as soon as our job here is done.

Yeah, Merry Christmas Michigan and my Grand Rapidian friends both living and unliving. We'll see you in a few if the good Lord and a few well-placed lead rounds permit.

J.E.B.

GLOSSARY

HTV – Heavy Transport Vehicle

APC – Armored Personnel Carrier

LTV – Light Tactical Vehicle

BRV-O – Blast Resistant Vehicle-Off Road, a LTV to replace the Humvee

OP – Outpost, e.g. Bridge Street OP

MDZ – Meat Drop Zone

GRCC – Grand Rapids Central Command, a large military outfit headquartered in Grand Rapids

UCRA – Urban Civilian Retention Area, also Undead Civilian Retention Area (derogatory), the retention area located on the west side of Grand Rapids

NSC – North Shore Coalition, a region of small cities and towns and people spanning along the west coast of Michigan from Muskegon to Pigeon Lake, south of Grand Haven, the governing council resides in Muskegon

BTF – Butterworth Test Facility, where ZT's are patched up, if possible, and integrated back into service

FZ – Feral Zombie, the "wild dog" zombie/undead types who wander and hunt on the outskirts of fortified living populations and wilderness

ZT or ZiT – Zombie Trooper, military personnel who have been wounded in service but not killed dead-dead, and due to the vaccine they were given (see Datropoline) have turned to a semi-undead state retaining some, if not all, their training and military skills

H7N9 – the 2013 Bird Flu virus strain that became a global pandemic initiating the current zombie apocalypse

West Side Horde – a derogatory term for the UCRA undead

Bram, or Z-ration – the doped meat fed to the UCRA civilians to keep them "docile." It is also sold by the big city manufacturers to neighboring communities and is used as a diversionary tactic to feed rampaging Ferals long enough for the living populace to take other actions, ie, escape or arm up and destroy the "wild dogs" zombs

Datropoline – the name of the drug vaccine given to all the

military personnel after the onset of the H7N9 pandemic, later banned from legal use as a side effect was turning a person into a semi-undead state if they succumbed to the virus and did not die outright

About the Author

Peter Welmerink was born and raised on the west side of pre-apocalyptic Grand Rapids, Michigan. He writes Fantasy, Military SciFi, and other wanderings into action-adventure. His work has been published in ye olde wood pulp print and electronic-online publications. He is the co-author of the Viking berserker novel, BEDLAM UNLEASHED, written with Steven Shrewsbury. TRANSPORT is his first solo novel venture. He is married with a small barbarian tribe of three boys.

Find out more about his works and upcoming projects at:
www.peterwelmerink.com

Transcend reality with Seventh Star Press!

On the following pages we would like to introduce you to some of our titles featuring Sword and Sorcery, Post-Apocalyptic Fantasy, Epic Fantasy, YA Fantasy, and more!

To get more information on Seventh Star Press and our titles, please visit:

www.seventhstarpress.com

or connect with us at:
www.twitter.com/7thstarpress
www.facebook.com/seventhstarpress

Now Available from Seventh Star Press,
the horror stylings of
Michael West!

Trade Paperback ISBN: 9780983740209
eBook ISBN: 9780983740216

Trade Paperback ISBN: 9781937929718
eBook ISBN: 9781937929725

Trade Paperback ISBN: 9781937929954
eBook ISBN:9781937929831

Trade Paperback ISBN: 978-1-937929-18-3
eBook ISBN: 978-1-937929-19-0

Virtual Blue from R.J. Sullivan!

Softcover ISBN: 978-1-937929-32-9

eBook ISBN: 978-1-937929-33-6

Did you ever wish you could escape to a virtual world? What if you could...but then couldn't get out? Two years after her deadly clash with a vengeful ghost, Fiona "Blue" Shaefer still can't shake off the trauma of that night. Moving to New York with her father didn't help. Neither did absorbing herself in her college classes. Not even her poetry provided the solace it once did. She convinces herself that ending her relationship with Eugene "Chip" Farren, her long-distance boyfriend and final tie to the horrors of that night, might bring the closure she needs. Blue travels to Bloomington to break the news to Chip in person, but her timing couldn't be any worse. The Sisters of Baalina, vengeful cultists who practice a new form of "techno-magic," have targeted Chip's multi-player videogame as the perfect environment to cast a dangerous spell to free a demoness from the very pits of hell. In the process, their plan may trap Blue in a prison of the mind with no locks, no bars, and no escape.

Urban Fantasy from John F. Allen!
Meet Ivory Blaque!

Softcover: 978-1-937929-16-9
eBook: 978-1-937929-17-6

In The God Killers, the first book of The God Killers Legacy, former professional art thief Ivory Blaque is hired to procure a pair of antique pistols and gets much more than she bargained for when several attempts are made on her life.

Her client turns out to be a shadowy government agent who reveals that she is descended from a race of immortals, and that the pistols are linked to her unique heritage and the special psychic gifts she possesses. He uses the memory of her father to guilt her into working for him.

Ivory eventually gives in to his request, and in return, he presents her with her father's journal, which was written in an unbreakable code. Bishop believes that she is the only one capable of breaking the code and unlocking the plans of the vampire hierarchy. But when the city's top vampire is a sexy incubus with an attraction for her and she's assigned a hot new lycan enforcer to protect her, she finds herself caught between two sets of rock hard abs.

To regain her autonomy, clear her name, unlock the secrets of her past, and protect the lives of those closest to her, Ivory must play along with the forces trying to manipulate her. Ivory's life is rapidly spiraling out of control and headed for an explosive conclusion which she just might not survive.

Now available!   A Seventh Star Press Anthology
from editor Michael West!

eBook ISBN: 978-1-937929-69-5
Softcover ISBN: 978-1-937929-60-2

Vampires Don't Sparkle! poses the question: What would
you do if you had unlimited power and eternal life?

Would you...go back to high school? Attend the same classes
year after year, going through the pomp and circumstance
of one graduation after another, until you found the perfect
date to take to prom? Would you...spend your days moping
and brooding, finding your only joy in a game of baseball
on a stormy day? Or would you...do something else?

The authors of this collection have a few ideas; some fanciful,
some humorous, and some as dark as an endless night.

Join us, and discover what it truly means to be "vampyre."

From Bram Stoker Award-winning Editor Michael Knost!

Softcover ISBN:
978-1-937929-61-9
eBook ISBN:
978-1-937929-62-6

Writers Workshop of Science Fiction and Fantasy is a collection of essays and interviews by and with many of the movers-and-shakers in the industry. Each contributor covers the specific element of craft he or she excels in. Expect to find varying perspectives and viewpoints, which is why you many find differing opinions on any particular subject.

This is, after all, a collection of advice from professional storytellers. And no two writers have made it to the stage via the same journey-each has made his or her own path to success. And that's one of the strengths of this book. The reader is afforded the luxury of discovering various approaches and then is allowed to choose what works best for him or her.

Featuring essays and interviews with:
Neil Gaiman, Orson Scott Card, Ursula K. Le Guin, Alan Dean Foster, James Gunn, Tim Powers, Harry Turtledove, Larry Niven, Joe Haldeman, Kevin J. Anderson, Elizabeth Bear, Jay Lake, Nancy Kress, George Zebrowski, Pamela Sargent, Mike Resnick, Ellen Datlow, James Patrick Kelly, Jo Fletcher, Stanley Schmidt, Gordon Van Gelder, Lou Anders, Peter Crowther, Ann VanderMeer, Joh Joseph Adams, Nick Mamatas, Lucy A. Snyder, Alethea Kontis, Nisi Shawl, Jude-Marie Green, Nayad A. Monroe, G. Cameron Fuller, Jackie Gamber, Amanda DeBord, Max Miller, Jason Sizemore.

A Horror Anthology from
Editors Alexander S. Brown and Louise Myers!

Softcover: 978-1-937929-54-1
eBook: 978-1-937929-64-0

From the fiery abyss of the underworld comes 20 hellish tales from the south
and southwest. Within these charred pages are stories that will introduce you to
the many demons that stay hidden but are always nearby...

20 authors provide stories of possessed people, objects, houses, highways, and
the devil's favorite playground - the forest.

Dare to meet Deidless, a demon who is a buyer of souls. Discover what kind
of demons men can summon. Read of battles between good and evil. Learn of
ancient artifacts and stones that crave sacrifice. Finally, become acquainted with
legions of evil.

Again, we invite you, sit back, dim the lights, and prepare yourself to meet the
devils in the darkness.

Southern Haunts: Devils in the Darkness is the next in the exciting anthology
series that began with Southern Haunts: Spirits That Walk Among Us.